Dragon's Head

By R. G. BERG

Published by R. G. Berg

Wolf Shield - Progenies

Written by R. G. Berg

Edition 2022

Copyright 2022 R. G. Berg

ISBN 9798840234242

Cover Art: Stephen Berg.

Table of Contents

Chapter One

"I hate this place." Richard muttered for the "un-teenth" time as he scooped up another shovel-full of dirt and dumped it into the nearly filled hole. He stopped to sniffle back his tears and wiped his eyes with the back of his forearm. "Goodbye Shadow." he whispered, and he choked back a sob. Shadow was his dog and best friend for the past twelve years. "I'll miss you."

So much for small town hospitality: Richard was born in this tiny burg, but because his parents hadn't been, he was still viewed as an "outsider" by those whose families had been here for generations. He was ever so pleased to go off to university and join the ranks of strangers who accepted him as one of their own. He would have gladly spent the summer in Hamilton to find some two-bit job until the fall semester, but his parents had insisted that he return home. They pointed out that he'd save money coming home, as he wouldn't have to pay for a place to stay during the time off. Richard suspected they just really wanted to have him back with them. That was all well and good, until some local drunk t-boned their car with his truck and killed them both. As for the drunk, he staggered away down the road until the police picked him up.

Richard was still in the process of sorting out his parent's affairs when Shadow passed away in her sleep.

"Damn, I hate this place!" as he patted down the last of the dirt on Shadow's grave.

The breeze that filtered through the trees off the bay did little to cool his sweat-drenched body. Even though Shadow was a good-sized dog, Richard was determined to carry her, and the shovel, along through the trails that backed off the salt dock. This had been his and Shadow's playground and refuge of solitude. If he had his way he'd have buried his parents back here as well.

The rumble of thunder brought Richard's awareness back to the present. It had been a bright sunny day without a cloud in the sky. Now all was suddenly as if it were twilight, even though it was only midafternoon. The hair on his body crackled with static. The air was deathly still, but a distant rustle could be heard blowing his way. It grew in intensity as if a freight train had jumped the tracks and was about to roar down upon him. The calm air suddenly blasted him with gale force winds, nearly knocking him off balance. Rain drops the size of marbles stingingly pelted out of the black clouds. Lightning flashed and thunder exploded overhead. Instinctively Richard turned his back to the torrent and ran.

With the sheet of water slamming into his back, Richard dashed nearly blind, as much bouncing from tree to tree than actually navigating between them. The air shimmered blue before him, but he figured it was just a distortion of his senses – until all went quiet and black.

Chapter Two

Initially Richard thought he must have slammed into a tree. All was dark around him and there was none of the racket from the storm. But then there was the realization that he was aware of his surroundings. It was indeed night-time — stars sparkled in a black velvet sky dominated by a full moon. He stood in a forest clearing, and found himself within a low ring of greenish fire — no, a fairy ring of phosphorescent mushrooms.

This whole scenario did not make sense. Even if he had been knocked unconscious and now just came to after dark, he would not have done so standing on his feet — and there was no skull splitting headache he would have expected from head butting a tree. Besides, he knew that it was no time near to it being a full moon.

Hoping to gain some semblance of orientation, Richard scanned the stars overhead — not that he was up on astronomy, but he did know a few basic northern constellations. Although the stars were bright and distinct, he could not make out either of the big or little dippers, nor Orion's belt. Even the moon appeared larger, and he was sure that its surface lacked the familiar "man in the moon" patterning. After a while he started to become light headed and brought his gaze back to earth.

As Richard made a slow clock-wise scan of the surrounding forest, he became aware of the usual nocturnal woodland sounds; crickets, buzzing insects, even a distant owl hoot. At about three quarters of his circuit he noticed a light off in the distance. He had just made up his mind to head in that direction when a child's terrorized wail pierced the night. Instinctively Richard charged towards the bobbing light that also marked the source of the cry.

Repeated screams veered off to the right, so Richard tracked onto that course. Downhill he ran, the moon's light enabling him to avoid most pitfalls and trees. At one point Richard came down hard onto a dead tree branch that snapped under his weight. As he pushed himself off the ground, his hand came up with an arm's length section of wood. Hefting his improvised weapon, he again traced the agonized shrieks from the child.

The slope Richard descended levelled off onto a large open clearing. As he ran on he could make out the whimpering form of a young girl staggering his way. She stumbled, but quickly regained her feet as she glanced back over her shoulder.

A white glowing orb emerged from the trees behind her and she wailed "Whispey!" and began to cry. A second light materialized off to her right, and then a third to the left. Crumpling in defeat the girl slumped down where she was. The sound of Richard closing in elicited a despairing moan and the poor waif curled into a ball.

Richard knelt beside the child, and, at a loss for words, merely mumbled, "I'm here."

The girl reflexively rolled away in surprise and stared wide-eyed at the unexpected human voice. "Da?" She whispered, but then realized that she was looking upon a moon-illuminated stranger.

Without responding to her enquires, Richard rose to his full height and strode some five paces to stand protectively between the lass and the glowing spheres that had so terrorized her. What he was up against, let alone what he was going to do about them, he hadn't a clue. Richard readied his club like a baseball bat and glared at the blurry fireballs as they swayed in his direction.

It wasn't until the first orb came within ten strides away that it finally became distinct – a glowing skull carried upon a lumbering skeletal frame.

Richard gasped in fearful surprise and stepped back. Remembering the girl behind him he stood his ground and hefted his weapon threateningly, bellowing, "Get lost!"

Amazingly, the bony horror before him halted, however, the other two spectres continued on to encircle Richard between them all.

For lack of a better strategy, Richard took an initial quick step forward, pivoted suddenly left and charged the skeleton which had advanced from that direction. He swung his club at the glowing skull with what he hoped would be a homerun effort, but his target dodged out of reach. Along with a lack of impact, the swing's momentum resulted in the loss of both his balance and his only weapon.

Richard had the presence of mind to continue his role as he hit the ground, gaining purchase on both extended arms and one knee bent beneath him. Before he could push himself to his feet, a boney weight slammed unto his back and skeletal fingers grasped his neck.

A horrendous screech of agony erupted into the night. To Richard's amazement, it wasn't from him. The fleshless grips disarticulated into separating hand bones. The shimmering skull went dark and dropped to the ground before his downturned face. Other bone parts slithered off his back. As he leapt to his feet and turned to face his other protagonists, what remained of the whispey clattered into the grass.

As for the other two skeletons, they had simply frozen in place, as if not programmed to respond to just such an event. Both were in midstride, hands raised and jaws locked in a snarl.

Cautiously Richard approached the nearer whispey. At arms length he stopped, and reached out to touch its glowing forehead with his index finger. Again an anguished scream shattered the night's silence, the skull lost its glow, and all crumpled to the ground.

The remaining whispey reanimated, completed its step and turned to dash off. Richard was onto its back before it finished its second stride. Third time's the charm, and the previous results repeated.

Scanning the litter of moonlit bones, Richard shook his head. "Well Toto, it sure doesn't look like we're in Kansas anymore. But just where the hell are we?"

A rustle from behind caused him to start, and he sidestepped as he turned. To his relief it was only the girl timidly approaching him.

She was perhaps five years old, and had a petite build, with long black hair and dark eyes. Her only clothing was a tattered, soiled, nightshift. By the way she made her way towards him, he suspected her bare feet to be bruised, scraped and likely cut as well.

Richard closed the distance, and when he got within arm's length he sank to his knees and extended his hands. When she returned the gesture and clasped his fingers, the lass locked eyes with this stranger's.

"My name is Richard. What's yours?"

At that point the child released Richard's hands and flung herself towards him, slung both arms around his neck and buried her head beneath his chin. She erupted into a full tearful weeping.

Taken by surprise, Richard rocked back onto his haunches and gently held her in his arms. Eventually the crying eased to silence, but she didn't release her grip.

"My, my name is Sendra." She paused for a couple of breaths, and then eased back enough to again search out his eyes. "Are you a wizard?"

"Wizard?" Richard responded, confused. "I'm no wizard."

"But you killed the whispeys. Nobody but a wizard has the magic to do that. I don't think even my Da can do that."

"Magic? Nobody from where I'm from has magic, let alone they're being any wizards."

Sendra narrowed her eyes in confusion. "But everybody has some magic." She held out her right hand. "Look."

But to her surprise, nothing happened. Her brow furrowed in concentration, then she gasped as the same nothingness occurred.

Wiggling out of Richard's embrace she stepped back and again extended her arm with palm flattened upwards. A ball of fire erupted a span above her hand.

Richard shot backwards to catch himself on his extended arms, astonishment plain on his face. Sendra smiled and looked his way. "See." Then herself bewildered. "You blocked my magic. How?" Her face beamed with delight, "You are to a wizard!"

Richard worked his way back onto his knees. *"Could it be possible here?"* he thought to himself. Cautiously he mirrored the girl's outstretched hand and concentrated. Nothing happened. A second try, with the same result. Actually disappointed, "See, no magic."

Before he could lower his arm, Sendra reached out with her left arm and clasped Richard's fingers – and her fireball extinguished. "See, you are a wizard!"

"But, I didn't do anything." he stammered.

As if pointing out the obvious, "You blocked my magic with no effort at all. You must be a very powerful wizard to do that. I've never heard of anyone who could block magic. Maybe Da or Ma has? I doubt Marth would have."

The night's silence was suddenly broken by the caw of a distant bird, shortly answered by another closer by. Soon there were all kinds of other chirps and avian calls.

"Be morning soon." Sendra observed. "Da will be out looking for me when they find I'm not in bed or up and around."

Richard had just noticed that the moon had indeed travelled off further over the distant trees, and the darkness was lightening from the other horizon.

"Well, in that case, how 'bout we try to meet him part way?" Richard replied. "Let's have a look at those feet of yours first."

As he had expected, Sendra's feet were a mess. He was amazed that she had gotten as far as she had, let alone managed to limp her way to him following the battle with the whispeys. After a short explanation as to what he intended to do, he hefted the lass up piggyback style and followed her directions homeward.

On the way he got Sendra's story about what had happened that night. She had been woken up by the call of nature and was returning from the outhouse when she spied some fireflies just off of the path. She'd always loved watching them flashing in the night, and this time she was determined to bring some home. In her pursuit she found that they were always just out of reach. By the time she realized that she had lost track of where she was, she became aware of some really large lights off among the trees. Initially she watched to judge the best route to intercept these whopper fireflies, but then noticed that they were all coming her way. As these lights drew closer she realized that they were not the bugs she had been hunting. To her horror she recalled the tales her parents and grandparents had told her about whispeys – and what whispeys did to those they captured in the woods at night! Then there was her terrifying dash through the night-shrouded forest, climaxing with her fantastic rescue by Richard.

By the time Sendra had wound up her accounting of the night's events, the sun was just peaking through the far treetops. The distant call of Sendra's name by a male and two female voices prompted the lass's return shout of "Da," "Ma," and "Marth." Richard altered his course to intercept theirs.

In short order her father was in sight, and sprinted the final distance and swept Sendra up into his arms, off of Richard's back. With the removal of his burden, (even though the small girl seemed to weigh next to nothing), Richard felt the sudden grip of exhaustion. By the time the child's mother and sister arrived, Richard was on his knees, being supported by Sendra's father. After that, he couldn't recall how he ended up in the small tidy room, tucked into a felt mattress bed.

R. G. BERG

Chapter Three

Richard opened his eyes to a room flooded with sunlight streaming in through a pair of windows that pierced the cleanly whitewashed wall to his right. The chamber was furnished with a bed, a wooden chair and a small table that held an earthenware jug and a mug. Not that there was space for much else. A solid wooden door faced the foot of the bed.

Other than his running shoes, he was fully dressed. A fresh smelling sheet and comforter were pulled up to his chin, although his feet and ankles protruded from the end of a bed that was constructed too short for his stature. He had no idea how he had gotten here, wherever here was, but it sure felt nice. Richard brought his arms out from under the covers and groaned as he stretched to either side of his head.

The pounding of small feet clamoured up the hallway outside his door, accompanied by various voices yelling "Sendra, no!" "Sendra, stop!" and "Just leave him be Sendra!"

The door exploded open and a tiny figure attired in utilitarian dress flew across the room to land onto the bed, grappling his neck in a hug. Sendra squealed with delight, and "You're awake!"

Richard sat up, smiling, and patted the still clinging little cherub on the back.

Sendra's father appeared at the doorway, shortly joined by her mother. Richard waved to them. "Please, please come in. I don't know how I got here, but thank you so much."

"It is us who should be thanking you." Sendra's mother replied, as both parents approached to stand to the left of the bed.

"I'm so glad to have been of service. Oh, my name is Richard." and he extended his hand to the woman.

"Tina." she replied as she accepted the handshake. "Sendra's Ma."

The man then put out his hand, which Richard clasped. "Thomas,

Sendra's Da."

A wide-eyed girl of about fifteen peered around the doorframe.

"That's Marth!" Sendra piped in. "She's my sister. Come on in Marth! It's okay! This is Richard!"

But Marth barely shook her head negatively and slipped out of sight.

"She's just being shy with you being a wizard and all."

"Sendra. I'm not a wizard." Richard retorted.

"You are to. Right Da?"

Thomas pinked with embarrassment as the attention came his way. "Did you really banish three whispeys?"

Richard shrugged. "I don't really know. Didn't really do anything. The first one grabbed me and it just fell apart. The same happened to the other two when I touched them, but it's not like I willed it to happen or anything."

"The same with what you did to Sendra's hand fire?" her father asked.

"Yeah."

"Show me please." Thomas lifted his right hand palm upwards, and a small fireball materialized just above it.

Tentatively Richard raised his left hand to lightly cup it beneath Thomas's. The hand fire vanished on contact.

Eyes thoughtful, Thomas murmured, "I have never seen anything like that before." Peering over to his wife, she shook her head "no" as well. "I didn't even feel anything but your touch."

"Thomas, Tina," Richard spoke up, "Sendra said that everyone here has some magic. Is that true?"

Both nodded yes. "Never heard of anyone not." Thomas affirmed. "Different abilities and levels, but always with something."

Richard took a deep breath, not sure how his next train of thought was going to go over with Sendra's parents.

"I'm not from around here. I have no magical abilities. Nobody from where I'm from does."

Puzzled, Thomas asked, "Where is this land you are from?"

"Not land." Richard contradicted. "World. Your stars and moon are totally different from where I'm from. Somehow I've been transported from my world to yours. That must have something to do with how this world's magic reacts to me."

"See!" Sendra piped in. "That's what makes you a wizard here!"

"Guess it does." her father chuckled. "Be interesting to see how else magic reacts to you."

"It doesn't bother you that I'm from a totally different world than yours?" Richard questioned.

"You saved our daughter's life and soul." Tina responded. "For that we count you as a friend. And to have a wizard as a friend, no matter where he's from, is a double blessing."

"Come." Thomas coaxed. "You must be famished. Let's find you some food and drink."

Chapter Four

Richard sat on the bench along one side of the solidly built table. The common room contained two other such tables with benches that occupied the room between him and the presently blocked-open door to the courtyard. A freshening breeze drifted in though the windows that occupied the wall along with the door to the outside. To Richard's back was a large, door-less opening which accessed the kitchen.

While he enjoyed an improvised meal of cold meats, cheese and still warm bread, his hosts filled him in on their home and business. Thomas and Tina worked a farm, but also ran a small way station that provided modest sleeping rooms accommodating up to a dozen people, simple but filling meals and this common area for eating and socializing during the early evening. Travelers' horses would also be fed, watered and stabled for the night.

This cozy homestead bordered adjacent kingdoms far enough from either that neither bothered to lay claim to it, but it proved a handy rest area for those traveling between the two.

Having finished his repast, Richard was left alone to savour a steaming mug of tea and allowed to let settle what he had eaten.

Thomas had excused himself to go split wood for the fireplace and the kitchen stove. Richard had offered to help, but was thankfully declined by Thomas who insisted that there was only one axe. The others busied themselves in the kitchen behind him.

It wasn't long, however, that the racket of horses trotting into the courtyard interrupted Richard's peaceful contemplation. Thomas's voice could just be made out instructing the riders to go on inside while he attended to their mounts. Presently three men decked out in garish livery stomped into the common room. They carried themselves as to what Richard assumed to be soldiers. For some reason they gave him an uneasy feeling.

Marth appeared from the kitchen to attend the newcomers as they settled around the first table. Unsurprisingly, ale was ordered by the trio. As the girl turned to leave, the one on the inner bench backhandedly slapped her on the rump. All three roared with laughter as she scurried away. Face downcast and flushed, the lass hurried past Richard without looking his way.

Richard's attention was locked on the men, and his temper was simmering. He could feel his own cheeks warming beyond a flush.

Shortly Marth returned with a tray laden with mugs of foam headed ale. As she served out the refreshments, one of the men on the further side of the table gripped the girl by her left wrist. As she gasped, the butt slapper stood up to block her way back to the kitchen.

Richard snapped, and he roared "**Enough!**"

Startled, the seated men surged to their feet, knocking over their bench. The one already standing jumped aside and twirled around as if expecting an attack, hand to his sword.

Marth seized her chance and dashed for the kitchen.

As one, all three slowly slid swords from their scabbards, each muttering a variety of curses.

Richard slowly rose up from his own seat to stand at his full height. At six foot four inches, he stood a full foot taller than the larger one that faced him. As they followed his rise, Richard took some satisfaction as astonished eyebrows elevated at unexpectedly confronting a giant. He was also quite cognizant that he faced three naked blades while he was unarmed, let alone untrained to face even one swordsman - even if he had a weapon. Options narrowed to hurling his table their way, and going for the poker at the fireplace. Dashing back through the kitchen was not a consideration.

Just as he decided to act, a piping young voice screeched "Stop!" from behind him. Before he could prevent her, Sendra had planted herself at the end of his table.

"If you know what's good for you, you'd leave!" she commanded. "Richard here is a wizard. He killed three whispeys saving me. Would the three of you even think to take on one?"

It took them a moment to consider a likely bluff, and then the soldier who had slapped Marth sheathed his sword and waved to the others as they followed suite. Heads together, Richard could just make out something about the queen paying well for a new pet. The others chuckled and their leader turned to Richard with a smirk on his facer. He unfastened a pouch from his belt, loosened the drawstring and slipped his hand inside the sack.

"Okay wizard." as he pulled out his hand and let the bag drop to the floor. What draped from his upraised palm was what looked like a dozen or more curly ropes that appeared to have been much to large to have fit into the fabric container. The man lifted the thing to his lips and whispered to it. Richard's stomach did a double flop as the twine began to squirm and slither. "See if you can handle this!" and he hurled the writhing bundle at Richard.

Richard was too startled to react. As the living mass got within inches of him, however, the outstretched ropey tentacles repulsed from him and the whole thing shot back to its thrower. It snared and entangled not only him, but also his nearby companions.

By this point Thomas arrived on the run at the outer door, axe in hand. Stunned amazement played across his face, as this was obviously not what he had expected. Then he flashed a huge smile Richard's way. "Not a wizard you say?"

During this Richard moved to the end of his table and promptly took Sendra by the shoulders and directed her back towards the kitchen where Tina and Marth stood, gaping at what had just unfolded before them.

Sounds of gasping distress were being emitted from the trio by the time the "wizard" got to them. Arms and legs were all ensnared, and the coils were in the process of wrapping around their necks.

He squatted down so as all three could see his face. "Now, would you like to live?"

Eyes bulging as the tendrils slowly tightened, they vigorously nodded their heads and wheezed, "Yes!"

"Okay then. Before I free you, I'm going to curse you."

Their eyes managed to bulge open even bigger.

"First off, should any of you return here, you would die before you harm any of these people."

The tentacles constricted more as if to emphasize the threat.

"Second curse; should you send someone here to do them harm, your agent will return without doing their deed, and kill you."

More tentacle contraction produced more gasping.

"Now, before it's too late, do you understand and agree to these curses."

Gasps of "Yes!" accompanied with more spasmodic nodding.

"Okay then." Richard reached foreword and touched the tightening cords. Instantly all went slack and lifeless. The three captives hurriedly disentangled themselves and bolted out the door. Richard leaned over, snatched the thing off the floor, and followed the soldiers outside.

"Now," Richard spoke to the leader, "what was that about your queen paying for a new pet?"

Breaking his gaze from the tendrils that had nearly choked the life from him, he looked Richard's way as he continued to massage his neck. He bobbed his head before answering. "Her Majesty has an affinity for young, viral men. She would find you most interesting. It would have been well worth our while to introduce you to her."

"Ever thought of asking?"

The fellow simply shrugged his shoulders. "Considering the situation, my 'callie' seemed appropriate.

"Not that I'm interested in being one of your queen's play things, but I'll go with you, mostly to get the lot of you away from here. Keep in mind; the curses still stand! Now, go get your horses. We're leaving, **now**!"

The solder elevated his right eyebrow and lifted his hand as he took a step foreword.

In response Richard tilted his head to glare at the man, then straightened. "Not a chance. Get!"

The guy shrugged and followed his mates.

Richard turned and handed the callie to Thomas. "I want a chance to say goodbye to you all. Once we're gone, go burn this thing in a pit far from the house and then bury it. Better yet, dump a big rock on top of the ashes before you fill in the hole. Best have Tina along with a knife, just in case the thing still has some mischief in it."

"And what of those curses?" Thomas murmured for Richard's ears only.

Just as quietly, "So long as they think I'm actually a wizard, hopefully that should be enough to keep them away."

*

Even though Richard had made much of getting the soldiers all hitched up and ready to leave, it was nearly an hour before he was set to go.

Thomas handed him one of his weatherworn hooded travel cloaks. The farmer was ten inches shorter than Richard, but he was wide of shoulder so it fit fine that way, even if it rode up higher than it was meant to be. The farmer also provided him with a flint (his grandfather's talent didn't include fire magic) and a sheathed hunting knife. These were packed into a strapped travel tote bag. Finally he handed Richard an oak walking staff, banded at both ends with brass.

Tina came out with a good-sized cloth square in which she had wrapped a loaf of bread, some cheese and jerked meat, as well as a few apples. She had also included a hand-sized square of hardtack for when the bread was done. "This is for you wizard," she insisted, "not intended to be shared with the likes of those three." She also passed him a full, stoppered water-skin.

Thomas then warmly shook Richard's hand and patted him on the opposite shoulder. "Be safe now traveller, and we thank you more than we can ever provide for what you've done for us."

"The pleasure was all mine." Richard responded. "I'm glad to have been available to be of service when it was needed. And without meeting you all, I'd have been totally lost in this place."

Tina then took Richard into a hardy hug. "Like wise what my husband has said. You will always be welcome if you ever make it back this way."

"I'll be looking forward to that day." Richard nodded.

"And be careful around Queen Sionna." Tina warned. "She's noted for being an adept sorcerous, and not so benevolent as yourself."

Next approached Marth, and to Richard's surprise vigorously clamped her arms around his body, lifted her face to his and actually stared up into his eyes for the first time. "Thank you so much." She squeezed him once more and scurried over to stand with her parents, a shy smile on her face.

Sendra had tears flowing down her cheeks as she slowly sauntered towards Richard. When he dropped to his knees, she launched herself into his arms and wrapped hers around his neck. "I don't want you to leave!" she wailed. "I'm going to miss you so much!"

Richard wholeheartedly retuned her embrace. "I'm going to miss you too." Glancing up to the others, "All of you." He didn't ease off with his hug until Sendra's flow of tears ceased and she finally released his neck.

At that point Sendra took a step back, wiped away what remained of her tears, and smiled. "See that you come back wizard. Okay?"

His face cracked into a toothy grin, "Okay, I'll see what I can do. You mind you parents and be good until then. And no chasing fireflies, hear!"

"Deal." Sendra nodded.

"Deal." Richard affirmed. "Be safe now." He looked to the rest of the family. "All of you."

Rising again to his feet, Richard strolled towards the waiting mounted soldiers, turning to give a final wave fair well. Once he reached the fidgeting men, he piped up, "Okay! Move it out. Now!"

Chapter Five

Even though Richard's long strides set a descent human pace, he still slowed down the riders on their near pony sized mounts. Bort, the apparent leader of the trio, constantly grumbled and urged Richard to quicken it up. This badgering ceased with the giant's suggestion of switching places so that Bort could stretch his legs for a while.

"What's the hurry anyways?" Richard finally snapped. "You didn't seem to be in that much of a rush back at the way station."

"We were merely resting our horses and getting a quick drink." Bort replied.

"Got a bit distracted, didn't you?" Richard retorted. "And just what were you thinking on doing if that callie thing of yours had trussed me up? I doubt your mounts would have born my weight along with one of yours."

"There was a big workhorse in the stable there." Luke piped in.

Richard turned and gave Luke a deadly glare, to which the soldier dropped his gaze and turned away.

"And just what were you planning to pay Thomas for his only animal that worked his farm?" Richard directed towards Bort.

The lead soldier cleared his throat, and avoided the wizard's uncomfortable stare. Instead he reverted back to his initial topic. "We have vital documents to deliver to Queen Sionna from King Tanus."

"Leave Hal or Luke with me and go on to queenie with your so important papers."

Bort started with Richard's reference to "queenie." When his wide-eyed reaction to the term passed, he again cleared his throat and stated, "We need to stick together. Brigands may look to ambush one or two messengers, but tend to leave three soldiers alone. For one or two of us to show up with this information, the others had better be dead, or it'll be all three of our heads."

Richard gnawed on his lower lip as he mulled over what Bort had said. "Is this the only main road to the castle, town or whatever, we have to go to?"

"Yes." Bort replied. "To the capital where the Queen holds court."

"What about this? The three of you go and deliver your stuff, and return this way with a suitable mount that will carry my weight. I'll just keep following this road. I doubt bandits will bother with one traveler on foot. And if they do," Richard's tone deepened, "it'll be me they'll be dealing with."

"How do we know you'll actually be coming when we're out of sight?" Hal protested.

Richard gave him a level glare. "I'm walking with you now, aren't I? It's not as if you have me tied up and dragging behind that pony of yours. Your choice: Piss queenie off with being late, or chance that I may change my mind. Besides, where will I go?" (He didn't want to draw attention to the way station.) "I said that I'd come. All it means is that you'll have to wait for whatever reward queenie will give you for introducing me to her." Richard laughed. "That is if she doesn't have your heads for it in the end."

The three companions halted and grouped together as they conversed. Shortly Bort wheeled his mount to approach Richard. "We'll follow your suggestion and come back for you with another horse. We should meet up with you sometime on the fourth day from now."

"In that case, bring back some food." Richard suggested. "I'll be plenty hungry by then."

After a moments thought, Bort unfastened a sack from his saddle and tossed it to Richard. "That should help. It's only travel fare, but better than nothing on a growling stomach. We'll get by with sharing what the other two have stashed."

He then wheeled about and trotted back to his fellows. Turning in his saddle, he called back, "See you in four days!"

Hal add in his two cents, "And we'd better be finding you!"

To which Richard challenged, "Or you'd do what?"

Hal's eyes widened before he ducked his head and trotted off after Bort, who had just passed him by.

As the mounted soldiers disappeared around a bend, Richard added this new food allotment to his travel sack. That done he hefted his walking staff and commenced at a much more leisurely pace. He had thought himself in decent shape, but suspected that he was going to be stiff for the next couple of days.

*

The sun was just starting to slant through the treetops. Richard decided to stop early and set up some manner of camp. He was counting on needing time to gather firewood and figure out how to use an unfamiliar flint to start a fire. And he was right, as it was dark by the time he managed to nurse a spark into a sustainable flame. Once he had built up a healthy blaze, Richard pulled out and donned Thomas's travel cloak. He then made himself reasonably comfortable with his back up against a nearby log. It didn't take long for him to devour half of the loaf and a portion of the rations Tina had provided for him.

Stomach sated, Richard slouched down with his shoulders against the log and stared into the flames. Shortly after, he was snoring with his chin slumped onto his chest.

Chapter Six

Richard woke with a start, and groaned in pain. His legs were cramped from the previous day's unaccustomed pace, and his neck and shoulders knotted from sleeping against the log. He had no idea what had jarred him to awareness. But doubted that it was the predawn song of the birds.

The piercing, catlike screech convinced him that an earlier one was most likely the cause of his awakening. It was the following human scream and call for help that convinced Richard to ignore his protesting muscles and move. Using his walking stick he levered himself to his feet and snatched his travel sack as he hobbled past.

The horrors of the whispeys initially came to mind, but he quickly concluded that this was something different.

A feline yawl accompanied by more human crying launched him into a limping run. As he closed the distance he could make out a female voice calling out "Daddy! Help me!"

Cresting a treed rise, he came upon the scene of the commotion. A creature howled as it pawed and dug vigorously at the base of a tree. At first sight it appeared to be a lynx, but with a lighter build. As it savaged the ground Richard was surprised to note the extra long forelegs with bat like skin membranes that connected fore and hind paws.

Between the animal's exasperated snarls and yawls, Richard could still make out a girl's pleading for rescue. He surmised that she would have to be located below where the cat-thing was intently excavating, but how or where was not apparent. All the same, Richard issued his own challenging roar as he descended towards the beast.

The animal turned to face this unexpected assault, and snarled its own counter challenge.

Muscles limbered by movement and adrenaline, Richard dropped his travel bag and hefted the brass-banded staff in both hands and launched into a full-fledged blitzing attack.

Richard wasn't sure himself if he had been bluffing or was actually prepared for a fight, but the creature swivelled on its haunches, sprang off its hindquarters, and with all limbs fully extended, glided on tightly stretched skin membranes down the slope. Upon reaching the trunk of a large tree, it clamped onto the rough surface, climbed a number of feet, and then perched head downward like a squirrel. From there it glared back and snarled at its attacker.

Now Richard took pause to think things through. To him it didn't look as if the beast was actually ready to relinquish what it was after. If anything he got the impression that it was only preparing an aerial assault, and Richard wasn't so sure his staff could fend that off.

Walking stick still held at the ready, he scanned his surroundings. Where the animal had been digging, it had extracted a number of stones. Eyes locked on his opponent's glare Richard knelt down to retrieve a fist sized rock, and launched it at the animal as he lurched to his feet. Luck or talent, the projectile thudded off his target's left shoulder, causing it to mew in startled pain and loosen its grip on the tree.

As the beast scrambled to regain its hold, Richard snatched up a slightly larger stone. Taking three rushing strides forward, he roared, "Get!" as he fired off his second throw.

The rock missed its mark this time, splintering off bark just next to the animal's right ear. All the same, the animal reconsidered the situation, scurried to the tree's far side and took another gliding launch further down hill. Once it touched ground it continued on foot for a number of bounds and leapt for a third descending flight. It wasn't long and the threat was out of sight.

Hormonal rush ebbing, Richard sat back onto his haunches and took a number of deep breaths. Once the stars finally dissipated from his peripheral vision and his breathing calmed down, he turned to glance back to where the creature was so intently digging. A whimpering echoed from a small burrow that the cat's excavation had opened, but it was much to small for even a toddler to have taken refuge, let alone an older girl.

Then to Richard's amazement a tiny figure of a young woman stepped through the tunnel's entrance. Even if she weren't hunched over, fully upright she would not have stood more than nine inches tall. The diminutive lady peered to either side, and when she caught sight of Richard, momentarily halted, and then cautiously crept towards her left as if she expected that she couldn't be seen.

Richard took a deep breath, and then called "Hello missy."

She froze in place and slowly peered his way in horrified astonishment.

Finding the whole scene somewhat amusing, Richard chuckled and said, "Am I not supposed to see you or something?" But when she crumpled down and sorrowfully wept, he became concerned. "Don't be afraid. I won't hurt you."

At this point he was startled to notice that she sported a pair of translucent wings from the back of her shoulders, the left one creased and tattered.

"Are you hurt?" Richard called in concern as he hurried to where she had slumped. "Is there anything I can do?" He didn't dare touch her for fear of causing her more pain, but only squatted down slope so as to peer with his face at her level.

When there was no sign of intent on this giant's part to harm or entrap her, the tiny lass cautiously met his gaze. "You, you can see me?" she whispered.

Richard blinked as he sat back a touch. "Am I not supposed to?"

"No." she replied. "I should be invisible to humans, if I want to be. You are a human, aren't you?"

"That again." Richard thought. "Okay." He stopped to work this out. "Yes, I am human, but I'm not from this world. Where I come from there is no magic and for some reason magic here doesn't affect me. I take your invisibility does involve magic?"

Confused, "You're from another world? How can that be?"

"Kind of a long story that I'm not even sure of, but that can wait for later. My name is Richard." Cocking his head to one side. "Not wanting to sound rude or anything, but what are you? My world has no one like you."

"I'm a forest sprite. My name is Fae."

"Hello Fae." He greeted. Then returned his attention to her damaged wing. "That thing hurt you. Is there anything I can do to help?"

The sprite shifted to a more comfortable seated position and smoothed out her soiled knee length dress. "There is actually little pain with my wing, but I won't be able to fly back Home, and it will be a long walk there. My Da… ah father can fix up the wing easily enough."

Richard resolutely replied, "There is no way I'll be letting you walk any distance, let alone, with beasties like what nearly got you there. You point the way and I'll see that you get home safe."

The sprite searched this human's eyes, and bit her lip as if debating with herself as to how to respond. Then, "Daddy will not be pleased if I let you do this."

"Will he be any happier if we wait here until he shows up, whenever that happens?"

"He would have heard my plea, but likely be near dark by the time he would get here. And finding you waiting would not improve his mood."

"Then let 'Daddy' vent his spleen out on me. The closer I get you to home, the sooner he can get it out of his system."

Still looking concerned, Fae nodded her assent. "Thank you, Richard. I'll accept your help."

"Good then." as he regained his feet. "But first I need something to eat. There's not much of a selection, but you're welcome to whatever I have."

*

The odd companions travelled through the morning, chatting as they went. Fae perched easily on Richard's shoulder, which also allowed for easy conversation. The sprite recounted what had occurred that morning. The creature that had ambushed her while she was scouting out the state of the forest was called a "crax." Richard freely disclosed his "long story" and then attempted to explain about his world that relied on science with its absence of magic. Fae listened with wonder as he described machines that allowed humans to move across the land, through the sky and under the seas, and even into space to the moon and perhaps someday beyond. She still wasn't quite convinced that these "machines" weren't powered by some manner of magic.

The sun had travelled nearly a quarter of its arc past noon when Fae suddenly tensed and leapt to her feet upon Richard's shoulder as she yelled "Daddy! No!"

The human found himself suddenly surrounded by a half dozen flying sprites that materialized from behind trees and the undergrowth. One enraged bearded fellow hovered a yard before Richard's nose, raised his right arm above his head, and then heaved his hand to point at this human's eyes.

Fae gasped as all the circling sprites simply dropped out of the air and lay motionless on the forest turf. She stared in disbelief as the sound of multiple snores competed with the calls of nearby birds.

R. G. BERG

Chapter Seven

Richard knelt down to examine Fae's snoring father as she attempted to prod and shake him awake. Where as Fae more closely resembled Disney's Tinker Bell, her sire looked more like those ceramic garden gnomes – chubby, white bearded, but with wings. He wondered how he managed to fly – something akin to the bumblebee he guessed. (*"Maybe both relied on magic to stay aloft?"* he chuckled to himself). Fae must take after her mother, as there seemed to be little resemblance to her father.

"Here." Richard finally said. "Let's try this." as he pulled off the water-skin slung across his shoulder, and dribbled some of its contents onto the sprite's face.

Fae's father sputtered and choked as he abruptly sat upright and peered around. When his vision fell upon Richard he took a deep breath as his face went red.

Before he even got started, Richard crouched forward with a scowl on his face and nearly went nose to nose with the irate sprite. "Don't' even think of starting!" he bellowed. "Fae is hurt and needs your help!" Then in a stern tone, "You'd best listen to her before you consider saying anything nasty."

Having to stare into a working mouth lined with teeth the size of his fist that could quite literally bite his head off; the sprite went wide-eyed and pale. But then the giant's words sank in. "Fae's hurt?" he breathed with concern and looked her way.

His daughter turned to display her damaged left wing.

"Fae!" he cried and scrambled to his feet and spent the next couple of minutes examining and prodding the damaged member. "I can deal with this, but best wait until we get back Home. What happened?" which he followed with a nasty glare at Richard.

"Don't be blaming Richard for this." Fae cut him off sternly.

Then in a calmer tone, "I was attacked by a crax. Richard drove it off, and insisted on bringing me Home so that you can fix me up."

With astonishment in his eyes, "You drove off a crax? Those are nasty critters, even for a human. Haven't been one of those near here in a long time."

"If that impresses you Dad, he destroyed three whispeys to protect a human child." Fae said in a matter of fact tone.

"Whispeys? he said with awe. "Three of them?" Then concerned, "Fae, have you brought a wizard amongst us?"

"I am not a wizard!" Richard retorted, perhaps more harshly than he intended.

Even though her father flinched, Fae calmly said, "In this world, you certainty are."

Puzzled, her father stared at her. "This world? What do you mean by that?" Then looked Richard's way for an explanation.

It took some time for Richard to retell his story, including how his world differed from this one, and that he had no idea how he had managed to bridge the two.

"How long ago did this happen?" asked Fae's father.

Mystified by that, "Two? Yes, two nights ago." Richard responded.

"The Stone?" whispered the sprite thoughtfully. "May be nothing," he said to himself, "but maybe…?" He then shook his head. "Something for me to look into later." but he gave no further explanation.

"You claim to have no magic, then how did you defeat those whispeys?"

"Just by touching them. Actually, the first one grabbed me. They just fell apart on contact."

"Interesting. And if you can work no magic, how did you not only deflect my sleep spell, but rebounded it back to put the lot of us under it?"

"No idea." Richard answered. "Same thing happened when a soldier threw his callie at me. It just sort of bounced off me and attacked him. I didn't do anything to do that either. Though I did release him from it by just touching the thing."

"And Daddy," Fae joined in, "you may not have noticed, but he can see us, even through our invisibility spell. And he claims to do nothing to counter it either."

Fae's father shook his head, and then gave the human a sideways grin. "You deny any magic working, but believe me, here you'll rank as a very heavy weight wizard."

"But we need to get moving if we're to be Home before dark. By the way, my name is Bower. And considering our conversation, I take that yours is Richard. We may need use of that water-skin of yours to rouse the others."

After jolting the other sprites awake, Richard stood with a perplexed expression on his face. "My presence seems to present somewhat of a dilemma or threat to you. It would probably be easier on Fae for me to carry her home, but if it will ease your minds, I'll head back to the road myself."

"Daddy, no!" Fae quickly directed her father's way.

Thoughtful, Bower took up the offer. "Normally, that would be preferable." And he cut off his daughter with a glare. "But I'm convinced that you mean no ill intent towards us, and it would be beneficial for Fae to travel with you. Besides, it would be dark before you reached the road, let alone finding your way during the daylight may be difficult. And with a crax out there, even you, wizard, may be at risk in the dark. So please, join us for the night and we'll find you to your road in the morning."

A pleased grin spread across Richard's face. "Thank you. That is very hospitable of you." Presenting his hand palm up to Fae, "Come along my Lady. Time to mount your waiting steed."

R. G. BERG

Chapter Eight

On route to the sprite community Richard conversed with Bower, Fae, and a few of the others that were bold enough to join in. Of interest to Richard was the apparent animosity between humans and sprites. Bower explained that most humans looked upon sprites as a curious pet to show off to their fellows. A captive sprite was doomed to spend its considerable life span in a cage, with the threat of pain if it dared to use its invisibility spell to hide from being displayed.

That roused Richard's ire, responding that Fae was his friend and that he would never view her in that manner. And he would be honoured to extend the same to any other sprite he should come across.

Bower eyed him speculatively. "Thank you Richard. We'd be honoured to welcome you as a Sprite Friend."

*

Twilight was upon them and Richard's vision was having difficulty adjusting to the altering light level. At one point he wondered if his eyes were playing tricks on him, as they were sensing small blotches of light among the trees ahead of him.

Fae noticed his squinting as he scanned the forest before him. "Relax Richard. That's Home you're spying."

"Oh." Richard exclaimed and chuckled at himself. "What do you call this place?"

"Home, of course." she responded.

"That makes sense." as he shook his head. Thinking back, that's how Fae and Bower had earlier referred to it. Giving the sprite a sidelong grin, "I like that."

As they got closer, he could clearly make out patches of moss among the branches and at the base of tree trunks emitting a soft greenish glow, which intensified with the growing darkness. A thought crossed his mind and he slowed to a stop. "Bower. Am I going to scare the other sprites who are at Home?"

The elder sprite chuckled pleasantly. "Your concern is appreciated, but your presence among our party had been long noted by outlying scouts who would have forwarded news of your coming. Curiosity as to why you are with us will certainly draw everyone out to greet you."

Shortly after, Richard parted a wall of intertwining leafy branches, and stepped into a small clearing bathed in that soft green light. Tidy sprite sized shelters occupied the branches surrounding that open space. In the centre of the moss carpeted clearing was what initially looked like a curiously stacked campfire, but was constructed of foot long smooth white stones of about three inches in diameter. They were placed on end in a circle, leaning inwards and on a slight right tilting angle to rest their upper portions against each other. Bower passed over to this structure to hover above the stones, and turned to face in Richard's direction. Hands extended with palms down, he closed his eyes in concentration. The stony logs began to shimmer with a pale yellow glow, which intensified to emit a comforting white light and a warmth akin to a modest campfire. Richard was awed by the magic that this portly sprite must command.

Waving the human closer, Bower flew to his right shoulder to land next to Fae. He then addressed the assemblage of sprites who had accumulated amongst the surrounding branches and living structures. In a clear voice, Bower began. "I know you must all have many questions, but there is much that needs doing. I will try to keep things short and concise for now. The rest will be filled in later."

"First off, while on patrol, Fae was ambushed by a crax." A surprised murmur rippled through the crowd. "Her wing has been damaged, but nothing that I can't repair shortly."

Waving his hand to indicate Richard's presence. "Fortunately, this kindly wizard from afar was near at hand, and drove the beast off. He then carried Fae towards Home under her direction."

Open comments and questions began to be raised, some of which were not totally amicable, but the sprite leader hushed it immediately. "I have conversed with Richard here and am well satisfied with his benevolent intent. He has declared Fae his friend, and has extended that offer to all of us, and I in return have named him Sprite Friend."

A collective gasp and awe filtered down from the crowd.

"Now, like I said, things are needing attending to." Bower commanded. "Oakster!" He waved over a trim male sprite. "Gather whoever you think you deem needfull. Scour these woods and drive off this crax such that you believe it will reconsider ever returning."

He then called over a pair of matronly sprites of about his own age. "Snowdrop and Sage. Please attend to Richard's needs. It may take some doing, but see if you can scrounge up some food for our guest. And please make him comfortable beside the flame-stones." Turning a pleasant smile Richard's way, "Have no fear, ladies. I think you'll find this one kindly and thankful."

"And now Richard, please lower Fae to that door between those roots." which he indicated. "There I'll attend to her wing. It should be fine by morning. I'll come to you when I'm finished with that. There is something I wish to show you."

After setting Fae down, but before her father could usher her inside, Richard asked, "Is there anything I can do to help with this crax?"

Bower simply shook his head. "You'll want to be resting your bones for your journey tomorrow. As for the crax, Oakster and his crew can handle it, and they'll likely be gone for a few days harassing and driving that thing away to a point that it won't likely make its way back this way."

"So," the sprite straightened, "I'll leave you in the care of Snowdrop and Sage, and I'd best tend to Fae. I will check on you in a while." And he turned to his daughter and assisted her through the door.

*

The two old lady sprites fluttered speculatively around Richard, and then guided him beyond the trees that encircled the illuminated clearing. Shortly they came upon a cool spring that bubbled forth from beneath a moss covered outcropping of rock into a pool, and flowed off as a small stream. Here they suggested he drink his fill. Richard gratefully cupped up handfuls of the liquid, and then refilled his water-skin for later. During this period the three chatted, initially with cautious politeness, but by the time they returned to the flame-stones, they were chuckling merrily with each other.

Richard was directed to a flat-topped stone against a wide tree, which would serve as a low chair for him. Initially the pair of sprites were perplexed as to preparing enough food for a human of Richard's stature, but were relieved when he informed them that he had his own supply of edibles. However, they weren't all that impressed when he pulled out and started devouring the hardtack, jerky and a bruised apple. By the time he was brushing away the last of the crumbs, the sprite women had returned with a half dozen of sprite-sized loaves. The meal that he had just eaten had been filling enough, but he found the sweet and nutty morsels a pleasant desert to top it all off. He cheerily thanked the ladies.

Richard then pulled on his travel cloak and regained his seat, intending to rest back against the tree. However, Sage suggested that he might be more comfortable bedding down on the mossy floor before the flame-stones.

Surprisingly, he found the surface smooth, free of sticks or stones, and softly cushioned with the thick mat of moss. Richard made himself comfortably reclined on his back, and dozed off in short order.

*

Richard awakened, staring at the glowing moon, whose light was filtering down through the leafy branches above. Taking a deep breath he found his head clear and refreshed.

When he turned his head towards the flame-stones, he discovered Bower at eye level, also outstretched on his back with his hands pillowing the back of his head, and his face turned Richards way with a satisfied smile.

"Did you have a nice nap?" the sprite asked.

"Very restful, thank you. Has it been long?"

"Just long enough." Bower returned. "It gave me time for a rest myself after healing Fae's wing."

Richard inhaled deeply with concern in his eyes.

"And yes, she is doing fine." Fae's father answered before he could ask. "She too is resting well, and will be whole by morning."

"Now, I would like to show you what I had mentioned earlier. It may or may not have anything to do with your coming to this world, but the coincidence is interesting."

The sprite rose to his feet and Richard followed suite. Bower flew up and landed on his companion's shoulder, and then directed him where to go. The moonlight allowed the human to manoeuver the trail that he was guided to follow. They travelled down slope for a ways to come out upon a level clearing. Centred within this space was a stone monolith with a rounded point that stood half again Richard's height. The glow of the moon highlighted shadowed etchings of strange runes across the structure's surface.

Bower fluttered over to hover mid-distance between the stone and where Richard stood in curious awe.

"This," the sprite reverently declared, "is the Earth Stone." Glancing back Richard's way, "It began pulsing light twenty-eight nights prior to when you believe you were pulled to this world. The rhythm and brightness intensified each consecutive evening until it glowed continuously the night of your arrival. Since then it has been it's normal, inactive self."

Completing a mid-air turn to fully face Richard, Bower tilted his head. "Coincidence would you think?"

Richard had this impulsive urge to reach out and touch the Earth Stone, but also a thought in the back of his mind that it would be a bad idea. He purposely grasped his hands behind his back, and then responded to the sprite's question.

"Mighty big coincidence if it was. If you're thinking that this thing brought me to your world, why dump me where I saved Sendra from the whispeys, and not here?"

Bower glance down in thought, then back to meet Richard's confused stare. "Perhaps 'there' specifically to save the human child. And maybe timed to rescue my child as well. Perchance your 'non-magic' has a greater purpose here."

A shiver ran up Richard's spine. He was never much on the concept of fate, but the double occurrence of being in the right place at the right time to save another's life seemed to negate that these events were just being lucky random occurrences. "A 'greater purpose' may be a little strong, but hopefully whatever it is I'm doing here is something positive."

Bower brought Richard back to Home's clearing and bid him finish his sleep where he had rested before. As Richard reclined, the sprite dimmed the flame-stones to a faint glow, but the comforting warmth remained. Bidding each other a good rest, Bower departed to check on Fae.

Richard remained awake in thought, but eventually drifted off to a dream filled sleep he couldn't recall the next morning.

Chapter Nine

The now accustomed predawn bird song roused Richard from his restful slumber. He lay on his back, cushioned by the mossy mattress, staring up through the branches into the still dark sky. Awake and refreshed, he took a deep breath and decided to get up. As of yet there were no signs of any others about. Quietly Richard made his way back to the spring where he had drunk from the cool water. It took a bit to get up the nerve, but finally he ducked his head into the pool below the spring. It was but a heartbeat before he jerked back onto his haunches, gasping and sputtering. If he thought he had been refreshed earlier, he was certainly wide-eyed and awake now.

By the time he made his way back to the flame-stones clearing, the soft glow was replaced by the early morning's light. Sprites were attending to their dawn-time chores. Fae and her father had not yet made an appearance, but a blurry eyed Snowdrop and Sage commanded a small troupe of young sprites to cart out a supply of the small sweet loaves. There was enough to eat his fill for breakfast, and yet plenty left to stuff into his travel bag for later. He was overwhelmed, and frankly, embarrassed that these two elderly sprite maids had spent the night baking for his behalf. He repeatedly thanked them for their endeavour, and very, very gently hugged them to his cheek. In return they beamed merrily and were oh so happy to have done so, and pledged that they would gleefully do it again "when" he returned.

As the door opened that Bower had entered the night before, Richard was prepared to greet the father and daughter with a genial "good morning," but the solemn expression on the elder sprite's face stifled any comment. The absence of Fae hit his stomach like a lump of lead with a fear for her welfare. Richard's voice cracked with concern, "What …?" Then was totally confused when Fae finally emerged, wearing a hooded green cloak and toting a matching shoulder strapped travel bag. She flashed him a big sunny smile and fluttered up to land on his shoulder.

Now totally beyond understanding as to what was happening, he carefully knelt down before her father. Finally he managed to choke out "Bower, what is going on here?"

The sprite leader took a deep breath and lifted resigned eyes to meet Richard's. "Seeing as you saved Fae's life, she has decided to accompany you. This is a world strange to you, so she insists on assisting you on your journey.

There was silence as Richard let that sink in. Finally, "Bower. Fae. I expect no obligation on your part for what I did. That was totally freely given, and I'd do it again for no reciprocation."

Fae patted Richard on his neck, which drew his sideways attention. "I gathered that you would not presume to bind me for saving my life. This is now my wanting to come along with you as a friend. Unless, of course, you won't have me." That last came with a squint of her eyes that suggested more than a hint of challenge.

Richard scanned the treetops as he considered how he should respond to this situation.

It was Bower who paused him as the sprite uttered a warning tinged with humour, as well as resignation. "My daughter has a streak of stubbornness, quite like what her mother had. Best be careful how you answer her."

Richard peered down at Bower, who now stood with fists on his hips, and unsuccessfully restraining a grin.

The reluctant wizard breathed in deeply, exhaled and returned his gaze to Fae. Straight faced, "I can always use a friend." And gave her a big smile.

The sprite maid squealed and dived to attempt to hug Richard's massive neck.

"Okay then. Do you need to prepare anything more?" he asked.

"I'm all set to go!" Fae acknowledged.

"Fae can lead you back to the road." Bower called up.

"I'm sure she can, but would you care to join us that far?" Richard invited.

With that the sprite father returned an appreciative nod and flew up to join his daughter on the giant's shoulder.

*

By the time they reached the road, the sun was in the process of dipping beyond the trees. There had been something gnawing at Richard's mind during the walk, and decided to present it to the sprites.

"When I meet up with these soldiers, will they be able to see Fae if she is touching me? I'm afraid I may be putting her at risk if she stays with me."

Bower thought for a minute, then fluttered away to dodge behind a tree to appear higher up on the other side. "Can you see me now?" he called.

Bewildered, "Aw, yeah?" Richard answered.

The sprite returned to hover before Richard's face. "I would have been invisible to any other human, yet you can see me without your touch nullifying my magic. I would say that it is your own particular sight that allows you to see us."

"All the same," still concerned, "when we meet up with these guys we'd better take some precautions. They don't seem to have a high dose of scruples."

"We'll work something out." Fae proposed. "If things turn bad, I can always put them to sleep.

"You can do that?" Richard exclaimed.

Bower chuckled. "She is my daughter after all, and may have a few tricks that may be beyond me." Then he laughed, "Besides, if she cast a sleep spell at you, she might put an entire garrison to sleep. You'd just have to pick her up and carry her away and wake her somewhere else."

At this time Bower bid his daughter a final fair well and wished the pair a safe journey. It was nearly dark as he flew off back towards Home.

Fae managed to locate a spot where Richard would be somewhat comfortable. After a bite to eat they settled in for the night.

Chapter Ten

Two days later Richard joined up with Bort and his crew. Hal started off grumbling about having expected the wizard to have made better time, but hushed when Richard pointedly kicked a stone his way and glared at him.

Bort cleared his throat as Luke brought forward a tethered workhorse. "This should speed things up a bit for you. Afraid it was the best we could get that might bear your weight. Sorry, but there's no saddle near your size. I did manage to adapt a horse blanket with a cinch and stirrups so that you're not completely bareback.

This surprised Richard that the crusty soldier would have gone to the effort. When he offered his thanks as he took the reins, Bort actually smiled and nodded his head in acknowledgment.

Through it all, Fae remained in a crouch upon Richard's shoulder, keyed to spring into the air at the first sign of discovery. Fortunately the trio were oblivious to her presence, even after Richard had managed to mount his horse and "practiced" guiding it around and between the other three mounted men. When no one was looking she could feel Richard relax with obvious relief, and he glanced down at her with a smile on his face.

*

A fidgety Bort led Richard into a brightly lit receiving room. The man had developed a nervous twitch ever since they first trotted their horses through the capital's main gate, and his anxiety had increased with nearly each step towards the palace.

"Bort!" Richard finally snapped. "What is the matter with you? Is there something I should know?"

The soldier glanced nervously around the room, and unconvincingly shook his head negatively.

"Will there be trouble if things go sour between the queen and I?"

"Na, na, no. The Queen will find you quite fetching." Wide-eyed, the fellow rung his hands as he nervously paced in a circle.

"And if I don't find her so?"

At that, Bort snickered. "Believe me, nobody denies the Queen!" Realizing what he had said, he gasped and wildly scanned the whole room as if he expected a volley of arrows making a pincushion out of him.

"Don't count me out being a 'nobody'." Richard quipped, but his remark obviously went over the soldier's head, which he decided was just as well — he doubted Bort would have taken it as a joke.

When the door across the room cracked open, the clash of metal on metal erupted from the chamber beyond. Bort was waved forward and he scurried through, leaving Richard supposedly alone.

Coughing into his right hand, he whispered, "Are we being watched?"

Fae closed her eyes in concentration, and upon reopening them, directed his attention towards a wall tapestry hanging next to the fireplace.

Casually Richard looked about the room and moved to a chair against the wall opposite the hanging and sat. Without being obvious, his glance slowly passed over the heavy cloth, and he noticed a slight motion to the fabric that suggested that perhaps the wall wasn't solid behind it. Apparently someone was giving him the once-over before his audience with this queen.

The door reopened, and again the clang of steel flooded the room. Richard came to his feet as Bort appeared and beckoned him to the doorway.

Richard stopped dead and gaped at the scene as he passed into the huge gallery. Across the room was a raised dais with a single throne, occupied by an attractive blond woman he presumed to be the queen. Lining the walls were men decked out in plate metal armour, their helmets held in their arms, hands, or placed on the floor next to their fee. Initially the armour gave the impression of being medieval vintage, but on closer examination, the torsos had been hammered to take on the contours of muscular pecks and six packs.

However, what dominated Richard's attention was the two-person melee taking place in the centre of the throne room. In complete body hardware, a pair of these knights was going all out at each other with four-foot long broadswords. (an impressive feet as these fellow didn't stand much above five feet themselves). The remnants of shields littered the floor — the straps of one still flopped from the left forearm of one of the combatants. Evidence of these guys intent was obvious by the deep indentations and gashes upon their gaudy helmets and armour. This was not a mere competitive sparing, but a full-out lethal battle.

As the clank and bash of fighting continued, Richard leaned over to Bort's ear. "What's this all about?" he growled loud enough to be heard at close range.

Without loosing sight of the struggle, the soldier slightly turned to murmur back, "Sir Gee took offence to something Sir Fernando said about the Queen, so he challenged him to atone for his remark."

When that sank in, Richard asked incredulously, "They're out to kill each other over that?"

"Of course." was Bort's matter of fact reply. "Queen Sionna simply adores it when her favourites fuss over her like this."

"This is fuss?" Richard thought in shock. A closer examination of the woman across the way put a shiver up his spine. The queen was leaning forward on her throne with a gleeful anticipation on her face. *"And these are her favourites?"*

In the back of his mind, common sense dictated he not piss this woman off, but a stubborn streak reflecting an immediate dislike for the witch was dictating his attitude.

Upon the floor, exhaustion was evident with both combatants. Finally one of the knights misstepped. His opponent keyed to his advantage and with a spurt of energy, smashed his victim's sword downward and slashed a backhanded stroke that caught the man just under the right lower edge of his helmet. Blood gushed as the blade sliced into the spine and jammed there.

The half decapitated knight lowered to his knees, to then collapse onto his left side and flopped over onto his back, dragging the victor's sword with the weight of his steel plated body. The blade rocked upright like some macabre mast waving in the wind.

Richard choked back his gorge, but nearly lost it again when the victorious knight straightened up after panting back his breath, and clunked the short distance to his fallen ex-comrade. He then planted his left foot on the fellow's chest as he grasped hold of the sword's hilt and yanked the blade free.

Throughout it all there was total silence from the knightly audience. The only commotion heard were the squeals of delight from the queen as she rapidly drummed her slippered feet on the dais floor.

Bort leaned towards a stunned Richard and quietly breathed, "That's Sir

Gee still standing.

The whispered comment awakened Richard's realization that he had been holding his breath and was beginning to see stars as he was becoming lightheaded. He also became cognizant that Fae had her face buried against his cheek and quivering as she hugged him tightly. As he coaxed himself to breath, his temper began to rise.

The courtier who had initially called Bort out of the receiving room now waved him and Richard to follow. They skirted the wall away from the armoured corpse and proceeded towards the dais. As they approached, the victorious Sir Gee was kneeling before his Queen and, helmet removed, placing a kiss to the back of her hand. The monarch tenderly patted him on the back of his head, but her hungrily anticipatory smile was directed squarely upon Richard.

By the time the trio had reached the foot of the dais, Sir Gee was standing possessively back and to the right of the throne. Although Richard kept a dispassionate eye on Queen Sionna, he couldn't help but notice the visage of jealous scorn that radiated from the knight's face.

Both Bort and the courtier dropped to their knees and quaveringly planted their foreheads to the floorboards.

Richard pointedly set his feet shoulder width apart, straightened his back to full height, and met the queen eye to eye.

"Insolent cuss!" Sir Gee burst out, but before he could continue, the queen raised her right hand to silence him.

Her smile broadened as she leaned forward. "So Bort. This is the wizard you promised to bring to my court. Please rise and properly introduce us to each other."

The soldier hastily clambered to his feet, bobbed his head towards his monarch without fully looking into her face. "Your most splendid Royal Majesty, Queen Sionna, please let me introduce" and he turned to present Richard, "the Wizard Richard." Head bowed, he backed away and waited.

The queen casually looked Richard over as if she might a fine steed or piece of jewellery. Finally she addressed the soldier and courtier, and dismissed them to retire, to which they hastily scurried off.

"So Wizard Richard. Do you think you are worthy to become a member of my court and serve me?"

"Actually." Richard's ire was surfacing and getting the better of him. "I've only come here because Bort had asked me to meet with you. As to entering into your service, that was never discussed or considered."

Sir Gee's eyes bulged with indignation and he reached for the hilt of his sword as he initiated a step past the queen, but again she halted him. Her smile widened into a toothy grin as she smoothly rose from her throne.

Fae reached to grasp Richard's earlobe and whispered "Careful. She's cast an enchantment on all these knights and they believe that they love her. She's about to try the same on you."

Richard slightly nodded his acknowledgement of her warning, maintaining his gaze on Queen Sionna as she approached.

And as she did so, her head continued to tilt at a higher and higher angle. For someone who stood barely four and a half feet, the realization of this wizard's gigantic stature pleasantly awed her. "My, my! You are a tall one!" the queen gushed sensually as she got an arm's length away. "Let's see if we can persuade you to change your mind." and she reached out to stroke his left forearm.

And she lurched back with a surprised gasp and clutched her arms protectively across her chest as she hunched forward.

Sir Gee, perceiving that this stranger had spoken crudely to his "love," strode forward, bellowing "My Queen! I will stand back no more to allow such insolence in your presence! I challenge this barbarian to mortal combat!"

Belatedly common sense broke free to natter, *I told you so!"* to Richard's temper. He didn't even have his walking stick, having to leave it at the palace door as it had been considered a potential weapon in the presence of the queen – some threat with all this steel surrounding her. As the irate knight's armour clad boots pounded onto the floorboards, Richard's mind took into consideration the differences in height on his chances of connecting with a front kick to the chest of the shorter man before he was sliced up by the guy's sword.

Luckily Queen Sionna straightened to fix her glare upon her oncoming champion, who skidded to a barely controlled halt. Composing herself, she returned her attention to Richard.

"How fortunate for you that Sir Gee's impulse for challenges has saved your life, momentarily. For your obvious magical rejection to my offer to join my court, I was about order my personal guard to simply butcher you for dog meat. But now I'll get to watch Sir Gee chase you around the throne room and carve you up piece meal.

"So?" Richard responded coolly. "This grandiose knight of yours is going to 'honourably' cut down an unarmed man in a formally challenged mortal combat? How sporting."

"Not at all. You may select any weapon and armour you like from the Royal Armoury."

Richard pointedly spread his arms as he glance down at his body. "And what in your tinker shop is going to appropriately adorn me. If I'm to match weapons and armour with this 'noble warrior', at least grant me time and access to a weapons-grade blacksmith. Or as challenged, allow me to choose the method of combat."

The queen narrowed her eyes. "And just what would you be proposing?"

"Magic at twenty paces?" Richard bluffed as he dramatically raised his eyebrows.

Slowly she shook her head negatively. "No magic, but I will concede to the services of an amply appropriate blacksmith, if you can convince him to do your bidding. I'll grant ten days to finish what weapon and armour you can manage to get made."

"Crap!" he thought. *"That sounds ominous."*

"Bort!" she called.

The soldier ran to her summons and repeated his earlier humbling position. "Yes, your Majesty?"

"Escort this 'wizard' to Gorm" (Richard clearly heard Bort's muffled gasp) "and let them work things out."

Chapter Eleven

Bort silently led Richard off deeper into the palace. He had expected to exit the main building to the stables, but after passing a heavy set of guarded doors, they descended stairs after stairs connected by dark, torch-lit passages to find themselves in what Richard would have expected to be the keep's dungeon.

Finally their journey ended at a high, wide planked door reinforced with iron strapping, fastened with heavy bolts. Thick hinges also testified to the weight of the door, and a large iron ring suggested to some strength was necessary to swing the thing open. A pair of torches secured to the opposite wall illuminated the portal.

Here Bort spoke for the first time. "This is Gorm's domain. May whatever god you pray to grant you luck dealing with that belligerent cur." With that he glanced Richard's way with a dejected grimace, and then turned to make his way back up the passage.

Richard stood and stared at the door for a minute, took a deep breath and peered over at Fae. "Just what the hell did I get us into?"

The sprite patted her friend on the neck. "At least nobody seems to have noticed me. I'm sure I can persuade enough guards to nap and pull a few tricks to get us out of here."

Cocking his head to the side, Richard took another close look at the door. "What kind of monstrosity would they need to shut up behind that thing? Then again…?" and he stepped forward and pulled on the ring. The door swung noiselessly with little effort on well-oiled hinges. That was totally unexpected, as well as the realization that such a reinforced gate showed no evidence of a locking mechanism.

"Well." he whispered to Fae. "We're here now, so we might as well find out what is up with Gorm."

The heat of a forge greeted them as they stepped through the portal.

Wide stairs descended straight down to a brightly illuminated doorway some two-dozen steps below. Considering this was supposedly a blacksmith shop, all was eerily quiet.

"Well, lets' get this done with." Richard said to Fae. Not wanting to risk startling whatever Gorm was, he called out loudly, "Hello Gorm! I need to talk to you!"

"Get lost dung head!" came the bellowed reply from below.

Richard chuckled. "Well that went well. I was starting to expect being greeted by an ogre or something."

"Oh, ogres aren't so bad." Fae returned. "At least not to sprites. They actually like humans." Turning Richard's way with a big grin, "With a side of toast and a mug of ale."

"Thanks." he laughed. "Let's go make friends." and started down the stairs.

Richard had to duck to get under the door's sill. A hammer whizzed past his shoulder to bounce off the stairs.

"I SAID …" started the earlier voice, which choked off as Richard entered the sweltering room to stand to his full height.

Across the way stood a figure near to half Richard's height, but with a torso nearly a third wider than his. Complete with overly full beard and biceps that would have made Arnold Schwarzenegger look small, what else but a dwarf would Queen Sionna's blacksmith be? Only the slack jawed stare of terror didn't seem to fit the image.

"Hello Gorm. Relax. I'm not going to eat you, but we do need to talk. And I really, really need your help."

The dwarf blinked, and realizing that his mouth was gaping, slowly closed it and swallowed. Clearly attempting to sort out what was happening, he turned and shuffled over to a chair and sat to stare back at the giant.

It was then that Richard first took note of the leg irons and chain that connected them.

There was silence, then Gorm seemed to regain a bit of his old gruffness. "Never seen no blasted human the likes as you. Let alone any of your kind with a pet sprite." as he glared at Fae.

That took Richard aback and he glanced over to Fae. "He can see you?"

She laughed. "Yeah. I figured you could use some back up."

"Just let me know ahead of time if you're going to make an appearance so I'm ready for it." He growled.

"Sorry." she replied unconvincingly. "Kind of a last second notion."

Richard focussed his attention back upon the dwarf. "First of all, let's get something straight. Fae here is no pet. She's my friend, and I won't condone any slight directed her way. Clear!"

Awed, Gorm thought this revelation through. "Don't that beat all? Could sure use a friend like that."

"And what would it take for us to be those friends?" Richard asked softly.

"That would be wishful thinking." The dwarf's head sank dejectedly. "Get these blasted magic bracelets off my ankles, and me out of this dung hole of a place, and I'd be a friend for life."

"Magic shackles?" Richard asked. "So that's why you can't cut them off?"

Gorm nodded his head sorrowfully.

"Magic in what way?"

"They're sealed on by the Queen, and only she can remove them. Anything I try to do to them is transferred ten fold to my ankles. Scratch a link or shackle, and it feels like a knife slicing my leg."

"Fae?" Richard consulted with the sprite. "Would you be able to get Gorm out of here?"

"I'd say there'd be a good chance, with a little luck on our side."

"What are you two going on about?" Gorm called over, disbelieving what he thought he heard.

Richard turned his way and paused before he started in. "Gorm, like I said, I really need your help. I kind of pissed of the queen, and Sir Gee has challenged me to a dual. I've bought some time convincing her that I need a weapon and armour suited to me to be built before I can provide a sporting fight. She's giving me ten days to convince you to forge it for me."

Gorm slowly shook his head. "Gee's a nasty grunt in a fight. Armour and sword would be impossible in that time."

"Forget armour." Richard countered. "I'll go as I am and hope to out manoeuver him in his steel suit coat. No sword either. I haven't seen anything like it here, but I'm figuring on a two handed mace built for my stature, so with my reach I can pound on him outside of Sir Gee's sword swing.

"What's a mace?" the dwarf asked, puzzled.

"Sort of a huge can-opener for those tins the knights like to wear around. I'll draw up something and let you do your magic on it."

"Can-opener aye?" Gorm chuckled. "Sounds something like a dwarf war hammer, up sized."

"But first, let's see what I can do with those shackles?" Richard stated.

Gorm's eyes went wide with horror and he jumped to his feet. "I thought you said Fae could get me out of here. I don't' want to be doing it hobbling on my knees!"

"Easy there Gorm." Fae soothed. My giant friend here is more than he appears. Richard is also a wizard. He specializes in nullifying magic."

Richard cautiously made his way Gorm's way. "The term wizard is still up for debate. All I'm going to do is touch your shackles and see what happens. If nothing, then Fae will try with you wearing them. However, I'm sure you'd rather walk out of here without those things, and I'm sure you'd work better that way too."

Slowly he knelt down to give the shackles a look over. Gorm was visibly shaking and closed his eyes as if bracing himself for the worse. Extending his hands, Richard gently laid his fingers around both metal bands.

The dwarf leapt into the air in response to the audible snip that resounded from the shackles, and the bracelets clattered to the stone floor. He crumpled to his knees on his impact back onto the ground and rolled over onto his rump – unbelievingly examining his ankles with both his eyes and fingers. Sniffling and unable to hold back tears, Gorm regained his feet and clamped Richard in a bear hug.

"Easy there Gorm!" Richard wheezed. "I may look the giant to you, but damn you dwarfs are strong!"

The dwarf whooped as he launched off the floor and then danced around the room.

"Think he's happy or something?" Richard grinned at Fae."

"Or something." Fae grinned back.

*

Richard sketched out his concept of a medieval mace with some verbal explanation as to what was expected of it. The smith pondered the human's drawings and came up with his own recommendations. He simplified the multi-faceted club-like head to a triangular cross section resembling a prism.

He explained that the bladed edges would provide maximum pressure along its reinforced wedge, while the flat backsides can be used for a hammer-like blow. The wedge should have the effect on plate armour like an axe splitting wood. The hammer side could deliver a smashing blow to joints that may flatten them out, decreasing their wearer's mobility.

Next Gorm had him lifting and swinging ingots of iron of various weights to judge what mace head size he'd be able to effectively fight with. And then repeated the process with different lengths of wooden polls to estimate an appropriate handle. The dwarf explained that he would have to calculate the combination of the two before he'd start work on the actual weapon.

To say Richard was impressed would have been an understatement. His concept of an "antiquated" blacksmith quickly elevated to what he might have expected from a modern-day engineer.

Then Gorm broke into a devious grin. "I also have an added secret surprise for Gee." He scurried over to his sleeping cot, rummaged through the bedding and returned with a shiny black stone double the size of his massive fist. "When they captured me, I had just collected this." and he held it up for Richard's inspection. "They saw it as a useless piece of rock, so cared nothing that I would want to bring it with me. Fools! That stone has more value than any sparkly gem on this world."

Richard drew his hand over the smooth, polished surface. Thrilled with what he suspected, "Is that a meteorite? That is, it fell from the sky?"

Impressed with this human's intuitive guess, the smith's grin broadened. "Indeed it is. I watched it fall the night before, and spent the next day searching the mountain I knew it struck. When I'd found the crater it was nestled in, it was still warm to the touch. It'll take some doing to melt this down, but I may be one of a few who can manage to do it. "Watch." Gorm stepped back two paces, and as he extended the sky-stone on his palms, it rose to hover a foot above his hands. The dwarf then squinted in concentration, and the scent of heated metal permeated the air. The meteorite began to glow red.

The smith relaxed and allowed the ball of metal to regain its normal black sheen. Still levitated, he guided the dark orb to his workbench and allowed it to lower where its heat caused the heavy planking to smolder.

Richard's amazement was plain on his face. "And people think I'm a wizard. You move things without touching them, and super heat metal with you mind. I'm nothing compared to you! You're a true wizard."

"No, no my friend." Gorm responded with a shake of his head. "I'm a blacksmith with extra talents. I can also manipulate and shape softened and molten metals. Saves a lot of hammering on an anvil, though there is still some use to that."

Glancing over to the cooling stone, Richard gave it some consideration. "So, what do you have in mind with that thing?"

"That 'thing' is harder than any metal I've ever come across. Even with my abilities I'll have to forge it hotter than is needed to liquefy steel first, and then use my talents to push it to molten form. At that point I'll use my magic to shape it for the head of your mace, along with a shaft to take a handle. And with that my wizardly friend," Gorm smirked, "you'll pound Gee's steel breastplate as if it was made of lead."

"It's little wonder queenie's kept you spirited away down here." Richard said with awe, and then broke into a toothy smile. "And I'm ever so glad to count you as a friend. Hopefully this will save my skin and Fae can get you out of here."

*

The dwarf smith completed his project in five days. Even smelted and polished, the mace head maintained its black, shiny finish, giving it a definite ominous aspect. Gorm fitted it with a dense, yet flexible handle of oak, which he said would absorb shock better than a metal one. He did twine a mesh of the black metal to encase the upper shaft of the wood to protect it from sword cuts. Above the handgrip he fitted upward angled cross-guards to protect Richard's hands should a blade slide down the shaft.

The remainder of Richard's allotted time Gorm worked him into getting accustomed to the weapon's use. Many a suit of armour "commissioned" for the queen's favourites were battered to unrecognizable heaps of tattered metal. By the end of each day, Richard questioned if he'll be fit to fight when the time came, but he did note that each following morning found his stamina improved.

Chapter Twelve

On the appointed date there was nothing heard until the midday meal. The queen was holding a "Victory" banquet at sundown, just prior to the duel. They were informed that an appropriate "repast" would be sent down for Richard to share with the dwarf.

Richard read much into this missive. Delaying the fight until the evening was likely intended to wear on his nerves. The concept of holding a victory celebration prior to the duel with only one contender present was to emphasize that Richard was considered on the same level as a sacrificial lamb for the main event. The "appropriate" food was more than likely to be tainted with something to ensure he was not in top form for a fair fight.

If anything, the late timing just worked in their favour for Fae to orchestrate Gorm's escape in the dark, while Richard did his best to provide a further distraction. As for eating, Richard had other plans.

*

It had been allotted to a disheartened Bort to deliver the pair's evening fair. He was totally unprepared for the outcome.

"Bort!" Richard welcomed cheerfully. "Good to see you man." He relieved the soldier of his tray of food and handed it over to Gorm. When the wizard then hefted his peculiar weapon, Bort gulped in terror and his eyes bulged, but as his believed to be attacker strode past him and out the door to take the stairs three at a time, his fear turned to gape-mouthed bewilderment. "Come on Bort!' Richard called back. "We have a Victory dinner to get to. Let's nab whatever buddies you've got on our way to give me a proper escort."

Coming to his senses, Bort snapped his jaws shut and bounded after his supposed prisoner. Heaving for breath he finally caught up to a waiting

Richard at the top of the stairs.

"Figured I'd best wait for you, as I have no idea where the banquet is being held."

Puffing for air, Bort stammered, "The … the … Throne Room. But …"

"Lead on then!" Richard directed through a Cheshire-cat smile as he swung his guard in front of him and propelled the fellow down the hall. Even though the soldier was armed, he was totally unnerved being manhandled by this giant who was wielding such an outlandish weapon. Bort simply gave in and did as he was directed.

As Richard had hoped, each palace sentry they came upon was totally taken aback by a huffing Bort escorting a grinning, freewheeling giant who commanded them to join the party in the Throne Room. By the time he and his trailing "escorts" of bewildered guards reached the wide corridor outside the banquet, the festivities were in full swing. The pair of sentries stationed to either side of the wide open doors snapped to confused attention as more than a dozen of their fellows "followed" the giant they were not expecting until after the meal. They had no time to challenge the crowd as the parade burst past and entered the chamber.

The rowdy merrymaking ground to a stunned silence as the huge wizard stomped into the midst of the party.

"I see you've started without me!" Richard bellowed, no longer smiling. He slammed the head of the mace onto the floorboard, resounding in a splintering crash, and then rested both hand upon the end of the handle. Sweeping a scowl over the assemblage, he was secretly amused that every knight shrank back before his gaze. Finally Richard broke into a devious grin and strolled to the nearest table, and was joyfully satisfied that those seated there vacated for a half dozen seats to either side - all but for one lass who sat open mouthed and wide-eyed directly across from him. As he sat down and smiled at her, she passed out, face first, onto her platter of food. Richard surveyed the feast surrounding him, and he was sure that it would be safe to eat. Playing out his barbarian persona, he dug hugely into the fair abandoned before him.

After purposely cramming his mouth full of food and started chewing, he glanced up at the queen centred at the dais high table. There, Sionna was still half raised from her chair, mouth agape and working as if trying to say something. He gave her a big toothy grin, and then commenced chewing again while maintaining eye contact with the queen. Finally she composed herself and regained her seat. Tilting her head towards an enraged Sir Gee beside her, she snapped something his way, which settled the knight into a scowl.

Being as this was a banquet, all her knightly entourage was in court attire and wearing only ornamental swords. Without proper armour and battle class weaponry, Richard was sure that they all felt naked, and likely bewildered by the unfamiliar devise he had laid before him on the table. Even Sir Gee was in light court garb, which suggested that he was going to require time to suite up for the duel – all the longer period for Fae to get Gorm away before his absence would be noted.

Finally the eating started to slacken off. When the Queen's Champion rose from the table and turned to request permission to retire so as to prepare for the duel, Richard also gained his feet. When he snatched up his mace and approached the dais, all in the chamber froze, including his challenger.

"Queen Sionna! Before your Champion departs to do whatever he needs doing for this event, we should clear up a few things before the match."

As Sir Gee straightened and moved to stand beside his sovereign, the Queen glared at Richard. "And just what, as you say, do we need to clear up?"

"From where I'm from, it is customary that when two knights face off against each other, the winner claims all possessions of his vanquished opponent. Is that agreeable?"

Queen Sionna blinked in astonishment, and then began to laugh. "Sir Gee, would you be interested in that, that thing that the wizard is pretending to be a weapon?"

The knight pondered the item in question, then "I can't imagine it being anything of use, but I suppose it would do for a curious wall ornament. Not that he'll have any use for anything when I'm done with him. Just what is it anyways?"

Richard was tempted to demonstrate its destructive potential on the nearby table, but decided to leave that a mystery until the battle.

"It's called a mace. And having been constructed by Gorm, it is far from useless." The reminder that the item in question was a product of the dwarf smith drew a serious, almost fearful, expression on the knight's face.

"Now," Richard pressed, "is that term agreeable?"

The Queen glanced at her Champion, who silently nodded affirmatively.

Returning her attention to this arrogant wizard, "Very well. Agreed."

Not wanting to let it go at that, Richard pushed to see what more he could gain out of this. "Seeing as you obviously consider this fight a foregone conclusion, I'd like to sweeten the pot should I win. For one, I would like that horse I arrived on. I've kind of grown fond of him."

"Fine." she conceded. "You can have that fleabag. And your other request?"

"A hundred gold coins."

"WHAT?" the Queen spat back incredulously. "That's ridiculous!"

"So, you do think I have a chance of beating this chump of a knight?"

Sir Gee looked about to launch himself over the table, but his Queen extended her arm to block him. Glaring dangerously at Richard, she replied through gritted teeth, "You'll have your coins, should you win. If you loose, I'll have your skin for book covers. That is, whatever's still useable after Sir Gee gets through with you." Beaming a sadistic smile, "Agreed?"

"Agreed." he replied evenly. "Just have the gold on hand for the fight, as I'll be leaving right after."

"Yes." she agreed. "I'm quite confident that it will be your soul departing once things are finished."

*

With the banquet over, the Throne Room was converted for the main event. Chairs occupied by partygoers lined the walls, with tables providing a buffering barrier separating spectators from the duelling combatants. A handful of giddy ladies sat upon chairs atop of the tables for a better view.

Richard paced the centre of the chamber with his mace resting on his shoulder. An hour or more had passed since his challenger had left to prepare for the fight. He was glad for the delay, buying Fae and Gorm further time to make their departure, but this dragging on was also getting on his nerves – that he didn't doubt was a deliberate tactic on his opponent's part. *'Just how long does it take these knights to squirm into their tin cans?"*

To occupy himself, and irritate queenie, (as payback), he would thud the mace's edge into the floorboards or drag circle marks on the wood. When the trumpets finally shrilled to announce Sir Gee's entrance, Richard was well willing and ready to get on with it.

The synchronized stomping of steel-clad feet marched through the main door and a disciplined double line of a dozen armoured knights parted left and right. As they in unison came to a holt with a final emphasized stomp, they turned inwards, clashed right steel sheathed fists to breastplates and extended them in salute. At that point Sir Gee confidently strode into the room within the honouring corridor of his comrades. Once beyond his fellow knights, he knelt to one knee and bowed in respectful homage to Queen Sionna.

"Rise my most precious and cherished Champion," she acknowledged, "and do retribution upon this arrogant barbarian for his slights."

As Sir Gee came to his feet and faced Richard, the other knights filed by to take up positions lined to either side of the Queen.

Richard sat the mace's head on the floor and let the handle lean against his body, freeing his hands to give a slow, casual clap. "Nicely done. Quite the entranced there, laddie. Though I think mine was much more casually intimate, don't you think?" Hefting his weapon and readied it as he might an axe to fell a tree. "Can we get on with this now?"

In response, the knight drew his sword, and purposely strode towards his adversary. When he got within ten feet away, he charged full tilt and his sword flashed.

Richard was unprepared for the speed that carried the iron clad Sir Gee so swiftly within striking distance. He just barely blocked the first blow with the mace's metal-laced shaft. He managed to step back to outdistance a second return stroke and block an expected back slash that caught onto the cross-guard Gorm had added to protect his hands on the handle. Richard twisted the shaft, trapping his opponent's blade from immediate disengagement. His karate classes came into play as he planted a sidekick that staggered the knight backwards three steps before he could regain his balance. In the meantime Richard backed off himself: lesson learned not to let his adversary gain such close quarters again. He was determined to carry things through on his own game plan.

Richard circled the knight counter clockwise, staying out of reach of the sword, but within range of the combined reach of the mace handle and his extended arms. This forced Sir Gee to continuously shuffle leftward to maintain his shield between them and not expose his back. It also placed the knight's sword furthest away from Richard. To counter the manoeuver, Sir Gee spun in the opposite direction to bring his weapon in a backhanded swipe. But even if Richard hadn't back-stepped, the blade was far out of range. As the knight finished the swing he raised his shield in defence of and expected counter attack.

And Richard heartedly obliged. Lunging forward he brought the edge of the mace down with full impact onto the upper quarter of the shield — splitting the entire length of its surface and slicing into the armoured vambrace behind it. The force brought Sir Gee to one knee. When Richard yanked the mace free, it pulled the knight forward, forcing him to catch himself with his sword hand, fist crashing onto the floor. Taking advantage, Richard swooped his mace behind, up and over to bring its flattened surface down upon his victim's right shoulder plates. The armour contorted and an audible gasp escaped through his adversary's helmet. He had to give Sir Gee credit in that he still maintained a grip on his weapon.

Richard stepped back, and when his opponent displayed no initiative to carry on the fight, he glanced up to the Queen on her throne. He expected an expression of shocked anguish. Instead she merely looked pissed off.

Shrugging, he stepped to stand before the knight's shield side, extended the mace to rest its head onto the floor, pulled back to pause it over his own right shoulder, and brought it around and up through a golf swing. The mace impacted the forehead surface of Sir Gee's helmet and sent the crumpled metal mass flying to crash some twenty feet away. Coincidentally, it settled before the dais in front of Sionna. As for the knight, he collapsed onto his back, eyelids fluttering in a daze.

Not risking his opponent playing possum, Richard used his mace to tap the base of the knight's sword blade, reassured when the weapon clattered to the floor and skidded a few feet away. Circling the motionless heap of armour, he crouched to retrieve the blade, and only then approached his fallen adversary from the top of the man's head. Resting the flat of the sword against Sir Gee's temple, he pushed the tip into the wooden floor.

Drawing his full attention upon the outraged queen, Richard flashed her a grin. "So, before I lay claim to Sir Gee's earthly possessions, the 'fleabag' horse in the stable, and that sack of gold by your chair, what might you offer for me to spare the life of your beloved Champion here?"

The noble Lady inhaled deeply, elevating her nose as if having sniffed something offensive. "A Champion defeated no longer deserves that title, and has no worth to me."

A heart anguished sob indicated that Sir Gee had regained his wits and overheard the whole conversation.

"So," Richard continued, "you have no use for this lad's life?"

"Non!" she snapped. "Do with him as you please, and be gone from my sight!"

"Very well." Richard drew the sword's point from the floor, and knelt down to rest the blade on the wood. He then cupped his free hand along the knight's tear streaked cheek. The touch shuddered the recipient's body, and the look in his eyes reflected confusion as if he had just awakened from a dreamy sleep. "I so also claim Sir Gee's life, and command him to follow me and be in my service from this time forward."

Richard locked eyes with the stunned knight and winked. In a whisper "Come with me and live. We'll discuss this later."

"Good then. Let's get you on your feet," and he assisted the man up, "and to your chamber to extract you from that tin can and collect your stuff." Turning back towards the dais, "And I'll be having those coins now."

Chapter Thirteen

It took Sir Gee only a short time to gather his belongings. It surprised Richard how little the knight actually had – everything was packed into a pair of saddlebags, and a special tote-sack for carting around his armour. Even his lodgings were somewhat more Spartan than he had expected that the Queen's Champion to have been afforded. She may have recruited hardy young playmates, but when out of sight she might as well have housed her "favourites" with their horses. The knight assured him that he still had a highbred warhorse and a pack animal, along with their gear, in the stable – which were now Richard's. Even with the necessity of prying the knight out of his dented armour, the pair reached the stable in less than an hour.

Fortunately, Sir Gee's two animals and Richard's horse were accommodated close together. Richard was about to open his mount's gate when Fae fluttered up from the other side and perched on the board before him. It struck him that if she was here, then …

The gate swung open and Gorm squeezed through. The knight froze in casting his saddle over the warhorse's back. "How…?" he began to stammer.

"That we can get to later." Richard cut him off. "Right now we need to get Gorm, and us, out of here."

"Yes Master." The knight answered as he dropped his eyes.

Richard sighed. "This we'd better clear up right now. Listen Sir Gee. All that nonsense I was spouting about claiming your life in servitude to me was strictly for Queen Sionna's benefit. I knew that you were under a spell that had you bound to her. I was only baiting her so that she would openly dismiss you before I broke her enchantment on. I have no use for a servant, and that includes you."

A dejected sigh escaped from the defeated knight.

"Look. I know I was awfully nasty in the way I treated you, and the trash talk I sent your way. Most of that was to irritate queenie there, but … I can be a real son of a bitch when I'm pissed off, and you were a handy target. I am sorry for all of that stuff I put you through. What I'm trying to say is that you are not my servant, but I sure could use all the friends I can get, and I'd like you to be one of them.

Sir Gee simply stared at him dumbfounded. Slowly, as realization dawned on what was just said, a smile slowly crept upon his face. "Thank you Mast..."

Whoa, right there!" Richard's hands shot up, fingers spread and palms forward, "Please, please, call me Richard. And if you don't mind, I'll call you Gee. By all means you still have your title, but I find this 'Sir' thing kind of annoying."

At that Gee laughed. "Fine then, as you will! I'll finish saddling your horse."

'Gee!" Richard interrupted. "This too I guess needs clearing up. That thing there is still your horse. I lay claim to none of your stuff. Again all that garbage was to irritate queenie. This here" as he patted the workhorse before him, "is my horse, as was bargained with her royal pain in the ass majesty. Come to think of it, about time I gave him a name." He moved into the stall and stroked its mane. "How 'bout George? Can you live with that?" he asked the animal.

"Aw, Richard." Gorm's deep voice drew all their attentions.

Bort stood in the doorway, his arms loaded down with stuff. "I figured I'd find you all here, Gorm included." as he indicated the dwarf with his chin. "I'd gone down to the smithy to let him know what had happened."

He moved into the midst of the stunned group. "Thought you'd be wanting this stuff." Bort deposited the pile onto the floor, and stood up and started handing some of it to Richard. "There's your walking staff, cloak and travel bag. I stopped by the kitchen to stuff it with as much travel rations as I could. I've also filled your water skin, along with two others. Nodding towards Gorm, "And there's this." as he lifted up the last item. "I figured that a smith might want a hammer, for one use or another." He hefted the largest mallet that he could find in the dwarf's workshop.

"Now, what do you say we get these beasties saddled up and you all out of here?" The soldier sauntered over and nabbed up a saddle off a stall's gate. "This should do for Gorm." As he turned with it, "What are you waiting for?" And he moved towards the knight's packhorse. "Her Ladyship is not the forgiving type, and once her fuming simmers back to thinking, she'll likely have everyone with a sword or pike out looking for your heads."

That snapped them all into motion to gear up. As Richard cinched up George, he called over his shoulder to Bort. "What about you? Will she be taking a strip out of your hide? Maybe you should be coming with us."

"Ha!" the soldier barked. "I'm nobody to 'queenie' there." and he turned a big grin Richard's way. "I only exist when she wants me to do something. And besides, it's you that has all her thoughts right now." His tone turned grave, "Anyways, I have responsibilities here." After a pause, "With her attention consumed with collecting your head, I'm likely safer away from you."

Finishing his task, Richard straightened. "Thank you Bort, for everything. I'm sorry for the times I made things tough for you too.

Bort laughed as he brought out Gorm's mount. "As I recall, it was kind of mutual at the time. I just kind of warmed up to you. Now, get lost, please!"

*

Having led the horses out into the courtyard, the trio mounted, and Fae took her usual place on Richard's shoulder, still only visible to him.

"How are we going to get Gorm out the palace gate?" Gee whispered, concerned.

Richard glanced at Fae, who quietly said into his ear, "I'll take care of it, but it'll have to be quick." The sprite fluttered over to land on the dwarf's shoulder, which gave him a start, but settled when she spoke to him. Gorm hunched over the horse's back, and disappeared.

Gee gasped, but Richard snapped. "Move! It won't last long!"

The knight turned and urged his mount into a trot, followed closely by the tethered packhorse, and then Richard's. The sentries stood aside as the party exited through the portal.

*

Once out of the city, the company took the left hand road at the second intersection beyond the gates. The partial moon still afforded sufficient light for the horses to maintain a steady trot on the packed earth roadway.

Even though Fae had managed to make the dwarf "disappear" again as they passed through the city's outer gate, Richard suspected that it would be noted which direction the arrogant wizard and disgraced knight had taken. It took them an hour before he was comfortable they could no longer be spied from the city battlements. At this point he directed the group onto a farmer's lane that cut between fields towards a forest. Upon reaching the tree line, they halted and climbed off of their mounts.

Richard could just barely make out the dwarf's form in the shadow of the forest and stumbled to his side. "Gorm, how is your eyesight in the dark?"

"My ancestors haven't worked the mines in generations, but I can still see nearly as well as in daylight. And yours?"

The tall human chuckled. "Likely just as blind as our friend Gee is. Can you spy a trail through this stuff?"

"Aye. Just off that way a few paces." (Richard could barely perceive the dwarf's hand pointing off to the right.) "There's a farmer's track he probably drives his wagon through to dump crop leavings. Should be fine to lead the horses by, but don't count on it going far."

"That'll be good. We just need to get back enough to be out of sight of the road."

The knight had joined them by this time. "Okay. We'd best walk the horses. You lead the way Gorm. Gee, you follow and I'll bring up the rear." (Richard figured his height, and Fae's own night vision, gave him some advantage.)

The trail did provide some spacing between the leafy bows to make travel not that difficult, but as the dwarf had predicted, it entered a small clearing occupied by piles of decomposing cornstalks. Beyond that there were openings between the trees, but no path, and totally black to the two humans' sight.

Holding back from the others, Richard whispered to Fae, "Are you able to glow the plants enough to light the way for me and Gee as we go?"

"Sure." she replied. "No problem"

"Thank you." And he cautiously led George over to the others. "Ah, Gee. I think it's about time we introduced you to the other member of our party. Fae, please give us some light and say high to our new friend."

The leaves above their heads slowly took on a soft glow that gradually intensified enough to illuminate the clearing. As the light level grew, the confusion on Gee's face became apparent, and turned to stunned disbelief when his eyes finally made out the sprite's presence on Richard's shoulder. Fae gave the knight a deep bow and a smiley wave upon straightening up.

"Sir Gee, this is my friend Fae. Gorm is already acquainted with her, and she knows who you are."

Dumbfounded, "Is, is that, … ah, she's, … a sprite?" he finally stammered out.

"Yes." Fae acknowledged. "I'm a forest sprite. Richard and Gorm are my friends, and I hope you will be my friend as well."

The knight nearly lost his balance and had to support himself against his charger. It took him several deep breaths to let it all sink in and gain his composure. Finally he gave a low chuckle and straightened up. "My life has taken quite the turn. I've lost the attentions of a rather nasty queen, to be befriended by a warrior wizard, a famous dwarf blacksmith, and now a lovely forest sprite. I do believe I can now die a very happy and contented man."

"Hey, hey! No dying on me now!" Richard admonished. "I've gone through to much to make you a friend." He laughed. "And knock off with that 'lovely' stuff. I saw her first. Literally."

"You never called me lovely." The sprite feigned a pout and leaned cross armed against Richard's neck.

Rolling his eyes, and glancing her way, "Well, you are lovely. Happy?"

"Just keep that in mind." as she laughed and patted his cheek. "You may have to remind me of it from time to time."

*

Their travel through the night shrouded forest worked out well. Gorm again led the way using his night vision. Fae maintained an umbrella of luminescent foliage that allowed the humans and the animals to safely follow the dwarf's trail. Well past midnight Gorm came upon a forest glen where they all agreed that they could settle down for the remainder of the night with little chance of being located by Queen Sionna's knights.

*

"Richard, wake up! Something's coming!" Fae called out as she yanked on his earlobe. He rolled over onto his knees and sprang to his feet as he nabbed the mace. The others had also sprung into action and made ready for a fight. The sprite had already put a small glow about the clearing: having considered that what ever tracked them in the dark already knew where they were.

At first Richard couldn't hear anything, but didn't doubt Fae's warning. Then the brutal crashing through the undergrowth and slapping of branches could be made out in the distance, but far to close for comfort, and unmistakably coming their way. A shrill squeal froze Richard's blood, echoed by a second, then a third.

"What the hell was that?" he breathed.

"The Were-Brothers." Gee answered. "This is not good."

"Were-Brothers? As in werewolves?"

"Shape shifters, yes, but not wolves. Maybe worse though."

There was another chorus of screeches, and much closer. Gorm hissed through his teeth. "I've heard somewhat of that crew. Nasty buggers."

"I've seen them, and what they can do to a fellow. Weasels nearly the size of you, Richard. Move damn fast. Three brothers: all homicidal bastards, even when in human form. Queen Sionna has them locked up until she needs them. Keeps those maniacs happy enough by tossing them people who displease her, which is a common occurrence." Gee pointedly looked Richard's way. "Watch your back as they'll often go for a hamstring first, but also get their kicks out of a gut wound and then drag out your innards."

"Real fun bunch." Richard murmured, also trying to judge the creatures' progress. "How do we deal with them?"

"As best as I can guess, we have to kill them out right. I've seen them take nasty wounds, but heal up right off. For me, likely go for taking their heads off with my sword. As for you two, bash in their brains. If you get one down with a headshot, keep pounding until you're sure they're dead, and then hit them again."

"Here." Gorm came to Richard's side. "Hold out you mace."

Without question, he raised his weapon. It took on a reddish glow, and then faded.

"Don't want to heat it up too much or it'll weaken the handle, but kill blow or not, I'll bet that'll cause some extra damage." The smith worked the same spell on his huge mallet.

"Fae," Richard called to her, "can you brighten things more so that we can see these things better?"

The clearing was drenched in near daylight brightness.

"Wow! Great! Now please get as high up as you can. I want you out of harm's way. If they tracked us by smell, I don't think your invisibility will keep you safe."

The sprite leaned her head against his ear and nodded. She then flew up into the tree branches.

They crowded the horses into the centre of the clearing. Gee's warhorse may stand a chance in defending itself, but the other two not likely. Then the men readied themselves with their backs to their mounts.

All went silent. Richard figured that this was just the calm before the storm, and not a reprieve. And he was right.

One of the giant black weasels burst full tilt out of the darkness at Richard, and a second launched from a nearby tree. He managed a blow to the jaw of his ground bound attacker, but the other bowled him over, and he nearly lost hold of his mace. The force rammed him into George's flank and bounced him onto his back beside the horse. The second beast landed with all four paws on the ground and leapt for Richard's face – to be met by a flying pair of hooves to the side of the head. Whether stunned or dead, Gorm followed Gee's advice and pulverized the weasel's head with his hammer until the skull and brains were an unrecognizable pulp.

A surprised but relieved Richard rolled over and gained one knee up. There, five paces away was his first assailant. His mace had caved in the creature's left jaw and side of the face, but to the human's horror, he watched the whole structure reconstruct to its original configuration – all the while the monster's blazing eyes were totally focused on Richard.

He knew he would never regain his feet in time to fend off the coming attack.

The were-beast crouched and leapt for its victim, to be jerked suddenly to the right and hauled over onto its side.

Though startled by this turn of events, both Richard and Gorm took full advantage of the situation. The friends alternated blows to the animal's skull.

Satisfied of their work, the heavily breathing pair scanned around for the third brother and Gee. To their relief the knight appeared from the other side of the horses, his sword smeared with blood.

Eyeing the two dead creatures, Gee smiled as he approached his comrades. "The advantage of having a trained warhorse. When that thing charged me, Rex lunged at it with his front hooves and gave me a chance for a killing blow. Took the head off in one swipe."

At that point Fae glided down to take up her familiar position on Richard's shoulder. He noted her big, satisfied gin, and got a hunch.

Stepping over behind his last attacker, he examined the hind legs. The tendrils of a tree root had entwined the beast's right ankle.

"I take that this was your doing?" as he gazed over at the sprite. She simply patted him on the neck and smiled. "And just how close did you have to get to do this?"

"Close enough." and she sweetened her smile.

Richard laughed. "Thank you. I guess that makes us even."

Straight faced, Fae came back with, "If we're keeping score, does this make it a game?"

"If it does," called over the dwarf, then Fae is in the lead! You both saved me, but I think my bashing that first Were-Brother even's me up with Richard."

"Great." Gee faked a grimace. "Guess that puts me in last."

*

Even being short of sleep, the adrenaline high and predawn racket of birds prompted the party to move on. Following the set up of the previous night, they pushed on through the forest. By the time that it was full daylight, they halted for a restful breakfast and a short nap before they continued on.

Chapter Fourteen

Come onto noon the companions came upon a narrow track. Following it they made better time. This trail eventually emptied onto an open field as the sun was perhaps a couple hours before setting. Not far from where they emerged were a half dozen labourers harvesting some manner of tuber crops.

As their horses came abreast of the workers, Gee halted and dismounted to approach one of the men to find out where they had come to. To his annoyance the fellow made no notion of acknowledging his presence. Even a not so subtle nudge on the shoulder got any response. Finally his temper got the better of him and Gee grabbed the man by the arm and swung the guy around to face him.

Gasping, the knight took two sudden steps backwards and reflexively reached for the hilt of his sword. The figure before Gee peered at him from an expressionless face through dull dead-like eyes. As if he hadn't been interrupted, the man turned away and resumed his task.

Trembling, Gee turned and quickly walked back to the others. As he related to his companions what had occurred, a man on horseback detached from the forest's edge not far away and casually approached the group.

"Good afternoon gentlemen. I am Lord Nemcro." Smirking Gee's way, "I see you've made acquaintance with my serfs."

"Serfs!" the knight exploded. "How do you claim lordship over dead men?"

"No, no, no. These fellows are not dead. There was a fever in the area a while back that did kill off a number of its victims. These are the unfortunates that survived. I have taken them in to work my lands, in return for feeding and caring for them. They require constant supervision and direction – otherwise they exist as little more than a tree stump."

Gorm levelled a sceptical glare Nemcro's way. "Care for them? I suppose a slave's tending may be considered being cared for by his master."

Stormy faced, Nemcro inhaled as he readied a rebuke to Gorm's comment, which altered to a speculative expression as he first realized the horsed speaker was a dwarf. In a mild voice, "You may well presume that these poor outcasts to be nothing but slaves, yet without my "tending" to them, as you so put it, they would waste away and perish. Given instruction, they would perform whatever task they are given until their bodies collapsed. It is my obligation to cease their work, to direct them to eat and drink, to sleep and awaken – all of which must be initiated and concluded by my guidance." The lord smiled. "Fostering children would be far less tedious."

The dwarf grunted, but left it at that.

"So my good fellows, as I have introduced myself, may I have the privilege of knowing your names?"

Gee caught Richard's slight nod, and the knight proceeded to name himself along with his titles. Gorm followed suit, though still with a bit of gruffness in his voice. Richard presented his name, but pointedly omitted his supposed wizardly status.

"Very good my Gents. I would much appreciate it if you will join me as my guests for this evening's repast. As you might guess, these poor fellows are somewhat lacking in providing much of a conversation." Nemcro chuckled. "I would well welcome your company. Gladly I offer you all a meal and accommodations for the night."

It was Gorm who spoke up, and in a genial tone of voice. "For a free meal and a clean bed!" and he laughed. "I'll mind my tongue and my manners."

"Splendid! Splendid!" Nemcro chuckled. "Just follow along this field to its corner and you will find the track that will lead you to the manor house. Tell Maggie, that's my cook and housekeeper, that I have invited you to sup with me, and that she is to direct you to the baths to freshen up while you await my arrival. I need a bit of time to walk these poor fellows back and see to their needs for the night."

*

Maggie hadn't so much as blinked an eye when the three strangers had passed on her lord's instructions. The cook/housekeeper showed them to an outbuilding constructed of stone blocks, and lit them a handful of lanterns before departing to prepare a meal for four.

An invisible Fae shadowed Maggie as she left, to wait outside the bathhouse.

Richard reflected on Nemcro's invite to "freshen up" as being a rather understatement. "Refreshing" would be closer to what he would have described it – if you consider plunging into a chilled pool refreshing. They filled the wooden tubs with buckets of well water. Bathing consisted of dunking ones-self in the bath, exiting to shiveringly soap up, and re-submerging to rinse off. A fire in the hearth might have been nice while he towelled himself dry – but at least he did feel clean.

*

By the time the comrades made their way back to the main house, Nemcro was there to greet them at the door himself. The lord cheerfully explained that other than Maggie and the serfs, he was the only other body available in the building. As Maggie was presently occupied in her cook's position, he was obliged to fill in as the doorman. He cordially led the way to the dining room.

As they entered the chamber, the cook was just placing the last of the meal onto the table and turned to exit.

The supper laid out consisted of some manner of sliced up roast, boiled tubers that the serfs had been harvesting, salad, and freshly baked buns. Goblets of wine had been poured and accompanied each plate and place setting.

"Please." The lord invited. "Sit and dig in. I'm not much on ceremony."

With that all present found a place at the table and commenced to fill their own plates and partake of the meal.

While Lord Nemcro casually engaged each member in small talk, Richard surreptitiously shaved off tiny pieces of his meal so that Fae could take her fill unnoticed.

Gorm and Gee sipped at their wine to wash down the food as they eat. Even the invisible forest sprite cupped a handful of the drink when Nemcro's attention was turned to one of the others. In time the dwarf and knight had to stifle yawns as the meal wound down. Fae had already nodded off, curled up under a crumpled napkin.

Their host contentedly pushed away his empty plate and reached for his goblet. "Well my friends! I thank you for your company. Before we leave the table, may I make a toast to Maggie for this most satisfying meal?"

The mismatched pair sitting on either side of the table raised and drained their cups. Richard however merely lifted his wine in solute and lowered it back onto the table.

Nemcro gave his guest a quizzical look as he too replaced his goblet. "Do you for some reason find my salutatory pledge to my cook somehow offensive?"

"No, no, not at all. I'm afraid that I have never cared for wine. Don't care for the taste, or its effects. Please take no offence. That's why I only raised my cup as a manner of recognition of you toast."

In quick succession, Gee and Gorm dropped their heads unto the table and noisily commenced snoring.

Wide-eyed, Richard glanced over to their host, and at that moment, realization clicked in that his cup was also untouched.

Lord Nemcro's countenance clouded as he glared at Richard, but shifted to amusement as he caulked his head to one side.

"I have never had a guest who has not enthusiastically partaken of a free offering of wine. This could prove to be most entertaining.

Suddenly Richard found both of his upper arms grasped from behind and he was pulled backwards over his overturned chair. Fortunately he managed to get his feet planted under him before his assailants could drag him to the floor. He managed to heave the man clutching his right arm to swing before him. But the fellow did not loose his grip, and Richard gasped on recognizing that it was one of Nemcro's serfs. Before he could take advantage of the move, an arm snaked across his throat from behind to pull him off balance, backwards. Two other of the serfs secured holds onto his upper thighs and heaved Richard's legs off of the floor. As he became horizontal, the grasp on his neck released, to join the sixth member in additionally restraining his lower arms.

An evil chuckle drew Richard's attention over his shoulder.

"This should prove to be most interesting. I've never performed the procedure on someone who is still awake."

*

Lord Nemcro's zombie-like servants followed their master, carting the struggling giant as if his weight hampered them not at all. Having acquired a lighted oil lamp, his path ventured down into the manner's basement to a wood panelled chamber. Richard was forced to sit onto a crude wooden chair – his arms and legs each restrained by a man while another immobilized his head with a chokehold from behind. During this, his captor further illuminated the room, kindling a half-dozen wall torches.

Whipping the taper to extinguish its flame, Nemcro sauntered towards his captive, with an anticipatory smirk on his face. "Well, well, well. This should be quite enthralling. I'll get to educate you during the whole process on just how I'm going to convert you into one of my mindless servants. I'll finally find out if it's painful or not."

The lord walked over and opened a cabinet along the wall, removing a sealed glass jar. Initially the container only appeared to contain a fist-sized glob of pinkish jelly, but as Nemcro again approached Richard's way, the inert mass began to quiver. Gelatinous projections formed on its surface, and further extended into pseudopod-like tentacles – attempting to reach the top of the container.

"This my friend is a very interesting parasite. I call it a brain-slaver. As far as I know, no one else has ever discovered one before, or at least survived its hosting, so I get to call it whatever I want." Nemcro raised the jar before his face and the creature clamorously stretched its arms his way. "You see, my pet is able to ooze itself through your nostrils and seep into the cranial cavity. As it absorbs your brain, it grows to fill its place, and thus takes over control of the your body."

Nemcro settled the vessel onto a table and unsheathed a tiny, sharp knife. "Now the trick is controlling these things, and thus I therefore control whoever it takes as a host."

As he carefully unscrewed the bottle's lid, the brain-slaver attempted to climb the glass walls. With a practiced swipe, Nemcro nicked his finger and drained a tiny trickle of his blood onto the blob, which was instantaneously absorbed. The tentacles relaxed and withdrew back into its mass. "By feeding this thing, I have formed a bond, and my magical gift is that the bond allows me to mentally command it to do my bidding. In return I provide nourishment and tend to its bodily needs." Turning his attention Richard's way, "And what a worker you and that dwarf will be!"

Gently Nemcro reached his hand into the jar and scooped his fingers beneath the parasite and elevated it out of its glass confinement. All the while the gelatinous critter remained passive. Cautiously he turned and gave

Richard a victorious sneer and proceeded to walk his way.

Richard attempted to break free, but accomplished only to waver his face a bit from side to side. His efforts just proved to elicit a chuckle from Nemcro as he approached nearer. The closer he came, the parasite animated to slowly extend and reach a cluster of narrow appendages aimed at Richard's face. As the creature was positioned a hand span away, Nemcro cupped Richard's head with his unoccupied palm.

With the touch, multiple reactions occurred. Richard felt the hands that restrained him give way. The parasite jerked, reversed its tendrils, and launched itself from Nemcro's hand to grasp onto his face.

Desperately Nemcro clasped onto the jelly wad, tore it away and heaved it to bounce off the nearby wall. As it splat onto the floor, he stumped on the organism and ground down with his heel.

A chorus of low growls caught the lord's attention, and as he looked up, he came to discover six hideously snarling faces — no longer possessed with listlessly enslaved eyes, but shining brightly with intelligently hateful malice. As his previously enthralled servants leaned to move his way, Nemcro screamed and dashed to the door, nocking the lantern to shatter against the wooden wall. Ignited oil slathered across the panels and commenced to consume the wood it soaked.

The freed brain-slaver infected bodies pursued their former master. Richard heard a pair of feet fleeing up the stairs that lead to the ground floor of the manner house, closely followed by the clatter of his multiple assailants.

A panicked screech testified to Nemcro not having made the door above, with thuds and banging accompanied with continuous wailing as he was dragged back to the subterranean corridor.

Richard made haste to exit the now smoke-filled burning chamber. As he worked his way along the passage wall to bypass the melee upon the floor, the flames from the room illuminated the bodies heaving upon the stone tiles. He came to realize that Nemcro's agonized peals of screaming were due to his attackers in fact gnawing off gobs of flesh and devouring them. Somehow he managed to hold down his earlier meal as he climbed the stairs on all fours.

The door above had been closed, which may have accounted for Nemcro not being able to make his escape. The smoke there was thick, and as Richard chokingly shoved open the portal, the stinking cloud rolled into the house proper, and he could feel a rush of fresh air suck past him down the stairs.

The resulting super heated air, that was triggered by a renewed supply of oxygen, roared along the passage and up the stairway, engulfing the bodies below. Richard was saved by his lowered stance on the floor, as the oncoming flames licked the ceiling above him.

He charged down the smoky hallway back to the dining room. He found Gorm on the floor, perched on his hands and knees, as he was already fighting of the drug's affects. First off, Richard located Fae, gently enveloped her in the napkin she had fallen asleep under, and cautiously tucked the sprite into the waist of his shirt. He then assisted the dwarf unto his feet and finally got across his muddled mind that they had to grab Gee and all get out of the burning building.

Shirking off Richard's assistance, Gorm hefted the knight onto his shoulders and effortlessly carried the knight out of the room and down the hall that led to the front door.

When they reached their exit, the smoke was thickly grey from floor to ceiling – stinging their eyes and making breathing chokingly difficult. The door was locked and they could find no mechanism that would open it. As Richard stepped back to make a running charge at the barrier, Gorm let Gee slip to the floor. With a two-hand swing over his head, the door's wood split down the centre. The paneled portal half exploded out into the night-shrouded courtyard as the other portion swung inwards, still attached to its hinges.

Once again slinging the knight over his shoulders, the dwarf led the way out of the building and away from the burning structure.

As they made their way to the barn where their horses were stabled, they came upon Maggie standing in shock, staring wide-eyed at the infernal that engulfed the manner house.

Richard reached to take her hand in an effort to draw her away, but the cook slapped it away. He tried again, attempting to verbally coax her to come with them.

"No." she croaked. "I have to find him."

"Maggie. If it's Lord Nemcro you mean, he's gone."

"No!" She turned to screech at Richard. "He can't be!"

"I saw the serfs eating him alive down in the basement. Then the fire burned them all."

Maggi thumped both fists on his chest and pushed him away. "You don't understand!" she screeched at him. "I have to go get him!"

"You can't Maggi!" Richard yelled back. "Everyone in there is burned to cinders!"

"You, you just don't understand." as she burst into tears. "He can't be dead. I, I have to get him out of there." Breaking into a screech, "He's my baby brother!" With that she broke away and sprinted to the flaming doorway and charged down the hall.

She had no sooner disappeared from sight that the entire structure collapsed inward upon itself.

*

Richard stared in bewilderment at the burning ruins, trying to fathom what had just happened.

After awhile Gorm gave him a nudge from behind. "Come on. This living carcass is getting heavy." Giving a nod to the barn, he turned and headed that way.

Richard took a final glance at the blaze, and then slowly followed the dwarf.

*

By the time Gorm had neared the barn door, Gee groaned and attempted to shift his weight on the dwarf's shoulders.

"Graw Gorm! You're cracking my ribs!"

The dwarf unceremoniously dumped the knight onto his buttocks. "You're not doing anything for my back either, you know." Tousling Gee's hair, "Good to see you back with the living."

The knight drew his knees up to his chest. "Looks like I missed something."

"So did I. I woke up enough to get your sorry arse out of there. Once Richard joins us, he'll have to fill us in."

The dwarf spit on the ground. "Damn! I was looking forward to a decent bed for the night."

Gee laughed, and patted Gorm on the stomach. "At least we got a decent meal. Guess we'll just have to make due with a bed of straw."

"You can go lie on straw if you like. Hay is softer, and less pokey."

Chapter Fifteen

It was early into the afternoon the next day when the friends broke from the forest onto a rough roadway. Turning right they followed the sun-dappled route. Shortly after, either side opened upon small fields growing a variety of crops. At this point Gorm called for a stop.

"Okay Gee, time for you to take the lead. Richard, you'd best move up and let me tag onto the rear."

Confused, the "outlander" was about to question the sudden change of arrangements, but Gee took up the smith's meaning. "Dwarfs are not common in these parts, and most humans look upon them as inferior beings. We're obviously into a populated region, and our friend will attract possibly not so amicable attention. For him to appear in an equal or even superior position could cause some nasty reactions."

Recalling Gorm's magical abilities and impressive blacksmithing skills, Richards' reaction was incredulous. "That's insane! If anything Gorm's more of a wizard than I am!"

"And that counted for what in Sionna's dungeon?" the dwarf responded. "The average human is no more sympathetic to non-humans than she was. Fae wouldn't fair any better, and more likely worse." (Richard's conversation with the sprite's father on this same topic came flooding back to his recollection.) "Animals will get better treatment."

This reminder triggered Richard's ire, but quickly sobered. "That really bothers me Gorm." Turning to Gee, "But I shouldn't be so judgmental. My own human history has demonstrated the same attitudes towards other humans, and in some cases, still do."

*

It wasn't far until a narrow river paralleled the track they followed, replacing the cultivation's to the right. Off ahead the glint of sunlight reflected from water that widened into a pond. Multiple streamers of smoke drifted lazily from thatched rooftops that clustered the further bank of the pool. As they neared, the companions could make out that a bridge spanned where a stream emptied into the open water from the pond's far end. The structure was ancient, but looked sound and well constructed with a low wall warding its outer lengths from the drop to the water. It was also the play centre for a number of the local boys who took turns demonstrating their "tightrope" skills upon the bridge's wall.

One of the older lads took note of the approaching party, shaded his eyes with a hand to give the newcomers a closer scrutiny. Suddenly he yelled and excitedly pointed. That caught the rests of the young crowd's attention, and a repeated chorus of "Dwarf! Dwarf!", could be made out by the riders.

Richard's temper began to smolder, but then he spotted a small boy clamouring onto the bridge's stone railing and wobbly come to his feet. A desperately bellowed "No!" silenced the dwarf calls, and the older boy made a dash for the youngster. Too late, the child with arms wind-milling toppled over the side into the water.

Richard thumped George hard with his heels and the pair rocketed past Gee on his charger. Whether the animal had sensed his rider's urgency, the workhorse surprised Richard with the speed with which he came to a gallop. During all this the wizard noted that while the others yelled and pointed to where their playmate had disappeared under the water, the older lad had sprinted to a nearby shack, and shortly emerged to be followed by a husky man still wearing a dark apron.

The fellow dived into the creek, coming up to stand chest deep. Scanning the depths, he made another plunge and surfaced with an immobile, soggy heap. Wading clumsily to shore he deposited the motionless youngster onto the riverbank.

George clambered across the bridge as its occupants scrambled out of his way. Gee followed close behind and Gorm shortly after. Richard launched himself from the horse's back and stumbled down the riverside to the pair below.

*

Brand was startled to glance up at the approaching giant, and coughed,

"He's drowned." He was even more taken aback when the stranger plunged onto his knees from the other side of the dead boy, and clamped a hand onto Dran's throat.

"Let me see what I can do about that!" the fellow murmured.

Brand's initial reaction was to slap the stranger's hand away, but as he lifted his arm, he heard the word "Sleep." and all went black.

*

Richard hurriedly checked for a pulse at the lad's throat. When the man across from him made to interfere, he croaked "Sleep." and without hesitation, Fae cast her sleep spell. The soggy chap slumped backward and snored.

As he had feared, there was nothing. Since the boy was already head down slope on the riverbank, Richard commenced chest compressions where he was. For the first half dozen heaves, water erupted from the lad's mouth and nose. By the tenth he switched to administer a couple of breaths, and returned to compressions.

A crowd of locals were gathering along the top of the bank, with Gorm and Gee planted between them and where Richard worked. "What are you doing?" the knight murmured his friend's way.

"Just keep everyone back!" Richard huffed as he laboured with compressions. "Hopefully I can bring him back. Explain later."

The watchers parted to admit a woman who shoved her way through. When she spotted the aproned man sprawled on his back and her boy being manhandled by a giant, she screamed and made to charge the monster.

The boy coughed, and the giant sat back. Another ragged choke vomited more water and he began to cry. The stranger lifted her son and carried him to the gaping woman.

*

Gee approached from behind. "I've never seen magic like that. Even healers can't bring back the dead."

Richard clapped the knight on the shoulder and steadied his weight there as he caught his breath. "That was no magic, and he wasn't quite dead." After a pause, "There are healers?" To which Gee nodded affirmatively. "We may need one yet."

Still breathing hard, Richard addressed the wide-eyed mother as she soothed the whimpering child. "Is there a healer here?"

She shook her head. "The town over. Why?"

"I brought him back from drowning," he responded, "but the boy took a lot of water into his lungs. That could be a problem I can't handle, and hopefully something a healer can."

The woman hip-cupped a sob. "He won't come here. Knows none in this village can pay what he would want."

"We'll see about that."

Gorm approached with the groggy, but congenially smiling fellow Fae had put to sleep. Richard was surprised to see the two behaving so amicable, which must have been apparent on his face.

"This here is Brand." the dwarf introduced. "Brand, this big wizard here is Richard," and nodding to the knight, "Sir Gee. Brand's a blacksmith, and smiths, be human or dwarf, share a bond."

*

As it turned out, Brand was the widow Brae's brother, and uncle to her son, Dran, who had inhaled all that water. It was Dran's older sibling, Drast, who had first noticed Richard's party and spied the "dwarf." He had also summoned Brand when all hell broke loose.

Following introductions (of course Fae remained out of sight) Richard had the horses cleared of their belongings. Calling his friends aside, he turned to the knight. "Gee, can you go look up this healer and bring him back." He handed the knight a gold coin. "Show the healer this, which he'll get if he comes right away." Another coin was passed over. "And he'll get a second for his services." Eyeing Gee seriously, "If he turns that down, tie him to a horse and bring him here."

When Gee asked for directions to the healer, Drast volunteered to guide the knight. Richard suggested that they take all the horses, and the boy instantly took a liking to George. The big workhorse was a gentle beast, and despite his size, was probably a good match for the lad. Richard again emphasized that there were to be no delays, no matter the time, and refusal was not an option. With that, Gee set Rex off into a trot matched by George with Drast, followed by the tethered packhorse.

Brae insisted that the wizard and dwarf take up residence with her and Dran for the night, which suited Richard fine as he wanted to keep a close watch on the boy – even though he wasn't sure what he could do if pneumonia or whatever set in. Brand, on the other hand, insisted that he offer professional courtesy in housing Gorm, who accepted happily. Considering the two homes were actually built up against each other with a connecting door, the differences as to who slept where didn't really matter.

*

The following morning Richard was awakened by the clash and bang of metal on metal. His startled, confused mind initially concluded that there was a battle, but as he lunged for his mace, realization that the rhythm was all wrong seeped into his mind. He chuckled as he flopped back onto Drast's cot, recalling that the two smiths had planned to get to work in Brand's forge – though Richard hadn't counted on their enthusiasm starting at first light.

The dwarf had requested if he could mend Gee's armour. He insisted that he'd make it better than when "he" had constructed it in the first place (seeing that the knight was now a friend). The human smith was more than accommodating, as he was eager to pick up whatever tips he might gain from a dwarf smith. Gorm estimated that his project would not take long, after which he promised to assist Brand with whatever work he had on hand.

Despite the din from the smithy, Richard dozed off again. It had been a long night, having been up a good portion of it watching over Dran with his mother. The boy was awake often from coughing fits. He started sweating profusely, drenching his nightshirt. All Richard could think to recommend was to sponge him down in a cool bath and have the boy constantly sipping water. It was nearly dawn by the time the sweats eased off and ceased, though there was still a mild fever. Exhausted, all three had settled in for some sleep.

*

It was the cessation of the bang and clang from the smith's shop that roused Richard a second time. His eyes snapped open with the felling that something was wrong. His hunch was shortly confirmed with the arrival of Fae, who had accompanied the dwarf to watch him work. "Richard! Quick!

Gorm's in trouble!"

Mace in hand, the wizard was on his feet and yanking the shack's outer door back on its hinges. Within the open yard between the smithy and the residences, Gorm stood defiantly, bare chested, his huge smith's mallet in hand, swinging the implement to fend off the half dozen spear points being tentatively jabbed his way. Brand stood with his back to the shop's outer wall, hammer in one hand and a still glowing set of tongs in the other, glaring at an armed trio of thugs barring his way to assist his fellow smith. Another eight men stood back brandishing a variety of weapons. One authoritative figure bellowed directions as he laughed and cursed. He rested a sword on one shoulder and a set of shackles draped over the other. This loudmouth drew Richard's attention, which confirmed to him that these hooligans were intent on taking the dwarf alive.

"Fae!" Richard addressed the sprite. "Go to Gorm and do your invisible thing."

Even though he could still see her, no one else noticed Fae zip to the dwarf's shoulder, and all in the yard gasped with the vanishing of their quarry. It struck Richard funny to watch the sprite point at the three spearmen between Gorm and their leader, and systematically spelled them to sleep. As an invisible Gorm approached the man, the sword he held glowed red and the fellow yelped as he jerked a burned hand away from a flaming hilt. The shackles' chain took on a life of their own as they snaked around his neck and lifted the startled fellow to stand upon the tips of his toes and suspended him there.

In the meantime Richard used the distraction to attack. He brained two spearmen before they noticed his presence. The final spear-bearer turned to discover a charging giant. With the man's surprised hesitation, Richard splintered the spear's shaft with a swing of the mace, and then shattered the fellow's shoulder on the backstroke.

Still invisible to all but Richard, Gorm and Fae made their way to those menacing Brand. The force of the dwarf's mallet smashed one man's spine as it propelled the body to bowl over the guy next to him. Brand felled his third assailant as the man stood stunned by what had occurred to his fellows.

Those remaining would have abandoned the scene, but their only exit from the chaos before them and the enclosing buildings was suddenly occupied by Gee on his charger. The knight and his warhorse made short work of the seven.

The companions, joined by Brand, converged on the only thug still standing (literally on the tips of his toes). Fae let Gorm reappear as he stood before the raiders' leader. As she did so, Gorm released his spell that levitated the shackles, and as the chain fell, so did the man to his knees to settle just below eye level of the smouldering dwarf. The expression on the man's face reflected the expectations that his would-be captive was about to tear his head off. Instead, Gorm lifted the chain from the man's neck, to shackle the fellow's hands behind his back.

"Who are these guys?" Gee asked Brand.

"The one now wearing the pretty bracelets is Krag. He killed his wife a while back. Nasty temper that one, when sober. Even worse drunk, and he was deep in his cups that night. Ran off and joined up with a bunch of other outcasts from around here, and worked them into a band of thugs and bandits. Whenever pickings along the roadways got lean, this pack would roust farmsteads or small communities like ours and take whatever they wanted. Places like ours were outmanned and out armed, so there wasn't much that we could do to stop them." The smith's face broke into a grin as he scanned the human wreckage that surrounded them. "You all have done the whole district a great boon!"

Despite their victory, something troubled Richard. "These guys obviously had Gorm targeted here. Someone in this village must have contact with Krag."

That train of thought was interrupted by the appearance of Brae, face all enraged as she tramped up to the bandit leader and slapped him across the face. "Brela disappeared two moons ago while out picking herbs and mushrooms in the forest!" I'll bet my soul that you had somewhat to do with her not returning!"

Krag leered up to meet her eyes and laughed. "Aye, and you'd be keeping that useless soul of yours. Your cousin had a disposition as fiery as your own. Took a week to break her, though after that she was useless doing chores and a disappointment in bed. So it wasn't that much of a loss when she just curled up and wasted away." Belatedly he realized that he had pushed Brand's sister too far as she took on an air of a snake about to strike.

And strike Brae did. She lunged to cup her palms to either side of the man's temples, and as she screeched her fury, a brilliant blue charge of energy discharged between her hands. Open mouthed in a soundless scream, Krag's body convulsed where he knelt, yet unable to escape the woman's assault. When smoke smelling of charred flesh curled from her victim's ears, Brae released the bandit to collapse onto the dirt.

The four comrades were stunned, though none would fault the woman, nor sympathize with Krag. Brand on the other hand merely shrugged, and turned to wave over his nephew, and the stranger frozen in horror who stood with him. Wide-eyed, Drast approached, but Brand, accompanied by Gee, were required to budge the newcomer to join the group.

"This here is Flaig, the healer we went to fetch." the knight introduced. Then in an agitated tone, "Didn't want to come before sunrise, but then demanded both gold pieces just to leave without his evening meal. And now wants double that for his services."

Feeling slighted, Flaig up tilted his nose. "I am a healer after all. I deserve compensation for my inconvenience, and my healing talents are of value." To give the man credit, he didn't flinch when the storm-eyed giant approached and glared down on him.

"Inconvenience?" Richard's ire was obvious in his tone. "This woman's child suffered through the night and may not survive another, so don't be blathering on about being inconvenienced to me!"

Eyes sparking with challenge locked with this out of place stranger. "And just who are you to question the likes of me?"

"Healer Flaig," Gee intervened, "may I introduce you to the Warrior Wizard Richard. You may want to reconsider your attitude in dealing with the 'likes' of him."

"Pa!" and Flaig turned his back to the wizard and crossed his arms. "I should just leave and let you see what happens."

"Two things will happen if you leave and Dran dies." Richard growled. "First, my major talent is dispelling other's of their magic." As the concept began to sink into the healer's contemplation, his eyes widened. "How much value will you have without your healing talents?" he bluffed. And Flaig's complexion visibly blanched.

"Secondly, you just witnessed what Mother Brae did to this bastard who pissed her off. Do you really want to chance letting her son die?"

Wobbly kneed and visibly shaken, Flaig turned towards the woman he had just witnessed fry another man's brain. Brae took the healer's hand and led him to where her needful son waited.

*

The sun was just dipping into the treetops when the healer finally exited Brae's home. Richard had insisted on overseeing the whole treatment of Dran, and would not release Flaig until he could hear with his own ear pressed to the boy's chest and back that the lad's lungs sounded clear. Even then Dran had to confirm that he felt totally fit and ready to run and play.

Flaig wearily stumbled up to Gee. "Please, Sir Knight. May I please gain your assistance in returning to my home?"

Glancing Drast's way, "Up for another night time romp?"

The lad broke into a brilliant grin and nodded affirmatively, and then scampered away with a whoop to begin readying the horses.

"I take that's a yes." as he smiled at the healer. Fishing his fingers in a pocket he extracted a pair of gold coins and presented them to Flaig, who just stupidly gazed upon them.

Richard, having followed Flaig out of the house, lifted the man's hand, palm up, into which the knight deposited the money. "Here is what you had asked for."

Almost in a panic, Flaig shook his head and acted to return the pay, but Richard pressed the hand closed. "Take the coins. And maybe another time you're needed, you'll be more concerned of someone else's welfare than what they owe you for your services."

*

That evening Gorm and Brand filled Richard in on the clean up of the morning's festivities. A good portion of the communities men and women turned out to aid in escorting the bandit survivors to haul off their dead and injured buddies to a distant ravine. The bodies were dumped into the crevice, and the remainder of the outlaws were then hanged along the gorge.

The matter of fact lynching took the wizard aback, seeming a bit of a Gestapo approach, However, he recognized the necessity here where there was no formal authority of law enforcement — these people had to protect their own.

Following that, it was not a difficult procedure to backtrack from where Krag's gang had been holed up. It was common consensus that the bandits may have useful items at their camp, some of which more than likely belonged to themselves. It was no surprise to Brand that one of their own had himself found the "rats' nest" well ahead of everyone else. A cousin of Krag's was apprehended exiting one of the brigand's hovels, pockets full, along with a sack over each shoulder, packed with valuables. Here was the informant who had tipped off Krag to a dwarf smith visiting the local hamlet. There was no opposition to allowing Gorm the honour of stringing the little snitch up.

Chapter Sixteen

They travelled three days along the winding road that cut through the forest until they came upon a T-intersection in their path. "Any idea where we are?" Richard asked the others.

Gorm shook his head, but Gee pondered, and then, "I think this about boarders with Sionna's realm. Drakeholm likely lies southward. Never been there though."

It was agreed that south was the safest destination, and Richard knew that Queen Sionna had been corresponding with King Tanus.

As the party road along, Richard finally gave Gee a close once over. He hadn't really noticed before but the knight was likely about an age with himself. It was obvious that the queen's recruitment requirements leaned heavily on looks and body build, with combat skill perhaps a lower priority, or simply a bonus. From observing Sir Gee's prowess in defeating Sir Fernando, it had surprised him that he had managed as well as he had against the Queen's Champion. Richard figured it was high time to actually get aquatinted with his new friend, and urged George beside Gee's mount.

After some ice breaking conversation, Richard's curiosity brought him to ask, "As I understand it, everyone here has some magical ability. What is yours?"

Puzzled, his companion glanced his way. "Odd question coming from a wizard. You make it sound to be different where you come from?"

That elicited a laugh from Richard. "Touché! Fae and Gorm already know my story, and I'll fill you in too, later. So, what's your thing?"

The knight whistled as he gazed up at the strip of blue sky peaking through the tree cover above. The look that crossed his features took on an embarrassed, guilty expression, and then glanced over sheepishly at Richard. "Knights are supposedly so all fired up on honour and such. I've always kind of felt my talent made me a cheater, even though I don't seem to have any control over it." Gee sighed. "It surfaces whenever I confront an opponent in battle. I … I. I sort of drain the other knight of his strength, and absorb it into myself.

"You looked all out of breath to me after you nearly took Sir Fernando's head off."

Gee's eyes elevated again. "All show. Just covering up my guilt." Then he turned full onto his new friend.

"But you! After that first flurry of blows, I could hardly keep on my feet. What did you do to me?"

It was Richard's turn to blush with guilt. But then he chuckled. "For one, your talent sounds like an excellent survival skill to me, and I don't seem to be all that different from you. This supposed 'wizard,' " as he patted himself on the chest, "has no control on what it is I actually do. I seem to nullify the magic of others, or rebound any magical attack back even stronger at the one throwing the spell."

From there Richard recounted his experiences involving the whispeys, Bort's callie, Fae's father, and the queen's "recruitment" attempt. "It looks like the same happened to you with our little 'tourney,' and I had no idea it even happened."

Then Richard described his own "magic-less" planet. Gee's eyes went round with amazement and his jaw dropped. He slowly shook his head as this "outlander" described how he had come to exchange worlds, and Fae's father's suspicion as to what had occurred.

After all was said, Gee reached over and gave Richard a comradely cuff on the shoulder. "You, my friend, are an amazing fellow."

"To me," Richard glanced at all his companions, "so are all of you."

*

Three more days and nights sheltered at shoddy way stations brought them within the kingdom of Drakeholm. Not for the first time did Richard thank his spur of the moment impulse to goad Queen Sionna to wager the hundred gold coins. Considering he received back a large sum of change for a single gold piece at the first night's lodgings, he'd count himself a fairly well off man.

The sun was a few hours before setting by the time the group rode through the main gate of Drakeholm's capital itself, and another hour to locate a respectable inn to spend the night. The presence of a dwarf drew some hard-eyed attention, but the companionship of a giant and a sword-toting knight discouraged any consideration of trouble. Of course, Fae went totally unnoticed. When Richard paid in advance for a suite of rooms and ordered up a hardy meal for the three of them, the party gained instant respect by the proprietor and his staff.

After they had eaten their fill, Richard opted to take advantage of the first decent bed since his stay with Thomas and Tina's way station. Fae nestled down into a feather pillow on a chair next to Richard, covered by a soft, fluffy towel. Gorm made himself comfortable by the fireplace, with the intent of sipping a pint of ale before heading off to sleep. Gee elected to visit the common room below to catch some of the local gossip and get the jest of the city's doings. A couple hours later a happily contented knight also retired for the evening.

*

The next morning the inn's owner timidly tapped on their outer door. Richard and Fae were already up and tending to their gear. Upon opening the door, they found a liveried officer with a high and mighty attitude standing behind the proprietor. But when the arrogant fellow had to crane his neck to meet Richard's eyes, his uppity airs dissipated to a more respectful demeanour. The appearance of a gruff dwarf hefting a massive hammer from one room and a courtly individual fastening on a battle worn broadsword arriving from another, elicited an audible swallow from the man. It was at that point that he noticed that the innkeeper had left him on his own.

Noting the apparent noble official's discomfort, Richard chuckled. "I have no idea what you've come to us for, but please step on in and do your thing." The trio stepped aside to clear room for the now jittery fellow to enter their common area.

The companions sat along three sides of the table. The messenger hesitated and stood at the unoccupied end, took a deep breath to begin, only to be interrupted by Richard.

"Please, have a seat with us and relax. Then tell us what you're here for."

The poor soul was totally at his wit's end. After being put in his place by what he initially expected were going to be peasants, he was now invited to be seated with them as equals, where he was accustomed to standing before his betters. Finally he shrugged and took the offered chair.

"Thank you good sirs. My name is Lord Cole, a Court Official to King Magnus. Word has made its way to His Majesty that a wizard has entered his city and taken residence within this establishment." Here he glanced the three over to gain confirmation and to ascertain which one of them was the wizard.

Richard sighed, as the other two looked his way. "Okay. Apparently that would be me." He pointedly glared at Gee, who smirked and found the ceiling very interesting. "Though, I'm still not totally comfortable with the whole thing."

That drew a confused look by the messenger, who again shrugged and continued on, addressing the giant directly. "Sir Wizard ..."

"Richard, please." he interrupted.

"Ah, Wizard Richard." (To which Richard rolled his eyes.) "His majesty cordially invites you to attend him at His court for the possibility of a position there in."

The reluctant "wizard" squinted his eyes as he stared at the messenger. "The last time I presented myself for a job interview at a court, I nearly got decapitated, and I'm still on the run from that one."

Gee laughed out loud and looked at his new friend. "Well, you did kind of provoke that."

The dwarf slumped down in his chair, crossing his fingers in front of him and murmured, "Psychotic bitch."

Fae had a difficult time holding back from snickering and making her presence known.

Finally, Richard glared at Cole, who obviously had no clue as to what had passed between these three. "Okay, seeing as you at least asked nicely, we'll" (and he glanced at his two observable companions, and subtlety included Fae) "come and see your King Magnus. Hopefully I won't be regretting it."

*

The throne room of King Magnus was not as large as that of Queen Sionna's, but then, to Richard's way of thinking, at least the guy must not use the space as a gladiatorial stage for blood sports. The ceiling was high and vaulted, with an enormous stained glass window depicting a rearing dragon with extended wings, which provided a glowing backdrop to the raised dais and throne.

Having been relieved of their weapons prior to being brought before royalty was getting to grate on his nerves. Richard was starting to develop a paranoia about appearing "defensively naked" before authority figures in this world, and would rather be prepared for a battle in case he had to make an exit from an unfriendly scene. Though, that may be what monarchs were trying to avoid by stripping "guests" powerless, as well as establishing their own superiority to visitors. All the same, he swallowed his irritation with the acknowledgment that at least things have been polite and courteous, so far. And this time he had Gee and Gorm with him, as well as Fae.

Lord Cole led the trio forward to the dais with a comfortable air of familiarity (in contrast to the atmosphere of fear and grovelling prevalent at queenie's court.), which boded well in Richard's estimate. As the courtier paused before the bearded, middle-aged gentleman perched on the throne, he gave a respectful bow, turned with a pleasant smile and gestured their way.

"Your Royal Majesty, may I introduce to you the Grand Wizard Richard, and his honourable companions, Sir Gee and Accomplished Dwarf Smith, Gorm.

As his friends imitated the Lord's bow, Richard figured that he could at least present this guy the same respectful gesture he would afford his karate Sensei within his dojo.

"Special guests," Lord Cole continued, "may I present to you the Sovereign of Drakeholm, His Royal Majesty, King Magnus!"

The King granted them a welcoming smile and with his hands cupping his knees, leaned their way. "Welcome Wizard Richard and esteemed Companions. I am most pleased and honoured that you accepted my invitation to consider my proposal."

"So far so good." Richard thought.

"Please, Your Majesty. Just call me Richard. I'm more comfortable with that.

Magnus grinned. "Very well then. I think we'll get along marvellously. Perhaps I'll get right down to why I've asked you here." His disposition altered to a discouraged seriousness. "My kingdom is in dreadful peril. For your successful service …"

As if on cue, a lovely lady in her late teens entered from a side door to approach the throne and lean against the side of its raised back.

"I will present you with the hand of my only child, the Princess Magnia, and make you heir to my realm upon my passing."

When the king paused, Richard's mind spun into action. *"Considering the reward, what the devil is this service he's expecting me to carry out?"*

As Magnus inhaled deeply to continue, the door on the opposite side of the dais crashed open to spill out an obviously outraged fellow – a couple inches taller than Gee, dark haired, perhaps mid-thirties, decked out in a swirling dark sparkly gown, pointy styled beard and a complexion to put a ripe tomato to shame.

"What the hell did I say about regretting coming here?" ran through Richard's mind.

As, what Richard guessed was "another" wizard, stomped towards him, Lord Cole nearly stumbled as he got out of the fellow's way and scurried to the chamber's wall.

"Your Majesty!" he shrieked, but pointedly locked eyes with what he assumed was his competition. "What is the meaning of this, ... this, ... interloper? I was of the impression that we had a contract!"

"Ah, well, yes Master Inkle." Magnus replied. "We had a verbal agreement. But when news of another wizard having come into my city, I wanted the opportunity to check out his competency for the job."

"Competency?" he nearly spat. "For my position?" and he raised his hands.

"Not a good idea Inkle." Richard tried to warn him.

"I'll show you his competency!" the rival wizard screamed.

Richard shook his head, closed his eyes and shielded Fae with his left hand.

Inkle whipped his palms forward to expel a glowing fireball at this contender. It impacted Richard full onto his chest – only to instantly rebound to its source, ten times its original size. Inkle was totally engulfed by the fireball, which exploded on impact.

The air snowed flakes of black ash. Princess Magnia had the presence of mind to dive behind her father's throne at the same time that Lord Cole had exited the scene. King Magnus upon his throne caught the full gust of the soot, causing him to hack and sneeze as he helplessly waved about his hands. By the time the air did clear, all that signified the existence of the irate wizard was a black smudge on the floor where he had stood, and the settling cloud of dark ash.

At this point the throne room was packed with armed guards that had dashed in, having responded to the sound of the explosion from within.

King Magnus did not look pleased.

*

The companions waited, not so patiently, in the throne room as the king and his daughter freshened up. Richard was tempted to just leave, but as the armed guards also remained in the chamber, bunched before all the exits, he got the impression that walking out wasn't going to be that simple. All the same, his tolerance was getting to the point of trying it anyway - when Lord Cole approached.

"His Majesty is prepared to see you now Wizard Richard." Eyeing the other two men, "Preferably in private this time, please."

Gorm and Gee both shrugged and wandered over to seats along one of the walls.

"Okay Cole," he growled, "let's get this interview over with."

The Court Official led the way to the door the princess had entered by earlier. The guards parted to let them through, barely, and Richard was quite aware that they also closed back in after they had passed. (*"Not a good sign."* he thought.)

Cole opened the door and politely allowed the wizard to enter, and then shut it behind Richard without coming through himself.

On scanning the small chamber, Richard came to question the king's concept of privacy. Princess Magnia waited near her pacing father, and the walls were lined with a dozen attentive knights. (*"Definitely not a good sign!"* came to mind.)

As Richard closed the distance between Magnus and himself, he decided to break the ice. "So, what's up?"

Magnus ceased his movement and drew himself to his full height, and inhaled deeply. He obviously was still not in a happy frame of mind. "What is up is that you just incinerated my only other wizard! Which now leaves you as our only hope for dealing with the kingdom's dilemma!"

"Whoa!" Richard interrupted. "For one, Inkle attacked me. Secondly, I still haven't the foggiest notion as to just what you are expecting for me to do, let alone whether I even want the job."

The king wandered over and sat down at the small table present and waved for the wizard to the chair across from him.

"As you know, my realm is called Drakeholm, drake being another term for dragon. The mountains south of us shelters a dragon that …"

"Wait, wait, wait a minute!" Richard cut in. "Dagon as in…?"

King Magnus flopped his hand back and forth, avoiding eye contact across the table. "Big, scaly, long necked, horns, large teeth, that kind of thing. Oh, and breaths fire. Did I mention huge body?"

When he sneaked a glance Richard's way, the wizard was giving him a hard glare. "The beast has been raiding farms, burning crops, devouring livestock, … the occasional farmer. Been getting a lot of complaints from locals of the area. Sending out knights and soldiers has been fruitless. The monster avoids them, or burns them to a crisp. That's why I've been wanting to recruit a wizard, and willing to offer my daughter and the kingdom itself for saving it."

"Now seeing as my only other candidate is a coating of ash spread around my throne room," as the king returned his own glare Richard's way, "I'm expecting that you will fill in for him!"

As Richard prepared to voice his objection, Magnus cut him off. "You have two options. Either hunt down the dragon and bring me its head while your friends remain here as my honoured, and very comfortable guests, or do the same with them locked away in the dungeon below."

Chapter Seventeen

As the mountains were a three-day journey, Richard elected to leave George back in the clean, dry stables of Drakeholm and ride on the wagon supplied to cart back the beast's head. He had figured the wagon would be more comfortable than the jury-rigged blanket-saddle anyway – only now he cursed himself for not thinking to cushion the wooden bench with a pillow. Or better yet, a mattress in the wagon bed until he could fill it with the creature's noggin. After three days, he was sure his backside was bruised and filled with splinters. At least Fae seemed to travel comfortably enough – except for the occasional pothole that would nearly jar her off his shoulder.

Magnus had supplied a contingent of fifty mounted soldiers, which the king figured would be enough to hull the dragon's head out of the forest and load it onto the wagon. Those men also made it abundantly clear, when the group had arrived at the foot of the mountains, that moving the prize was the extent of their orders. No one was to accompany and assist the wizard in his confrontation with the beast. So, should Richard be successful, he would have to return to camp, lead the soldiers back up to the carcass, and then walk back down again. He grumbled that he should have put in for extra mileage pay.

Two days of tramping the forested foothills proved to be a fruitless endeavour, and very exhausting. The bulk of the walking was up hill, but having to dip down slope and climb back up a higher incline made the journey all the more tiresome. If it weren't for Fae's company, he thought that he would have gone crazy by this point.

Late into the third afternoon they had finally reached the lower rugged slopes of the mountains themselves. As the sun was starting to set for the night, they came smack up to a chasm that was perhaps fifty feet across and possibly more than double that distance straight down. The landscape to either side ran fairly level for a mile or so, to then climbed and dropped steeply.

Richard and Fae scanned the area for a place to make camp before nightfall, but were stopped short by a distant howl of a wolf. An answering call confirmed that the animals were on the other side of the gap. But a third howl also suggested that the pack was coming their way, and closing quickly. By this time their ears were picking up the sounds of something large wildly crashing through the underbrush and lower branches on the far side, also approaching their way ahead of the wolves. It wasn't long until an antlerless deer emerged from the bushes and stumbled to a halt at the opposite edge of the cliff. Heaving deeply, the animal circled the narrow clearing, but from all sides came the snap and racket of its pursuers.

Richard watched in dread of what he suspected he was about to witness. But he was totally taken aback by the deer's desperation that led the animal to bolt full tilt at the chasm and leapt into open space as the first wolf broke cover.

The deer soared through the air, and dropped – only to stop, suspended in place.

Out of thin air a humongous creature materialized. A serpentine neck thick enough to swallow a Volkswagen Beatle soared twenty feet above the cliff's edge to end in a horned head with jaws that may well have accomplished the feat. One massive clawed paw had a grip on their side of the chasm. In the upturned palm of the other paw lay the motionless body of the deer.

Across the way the full pack of eight large wolves lined the cliff edge. Richard started as a voice sounded in his head. *"Sorry wolflings, but this poor animal called out for help, so I was obliged to assist. Good luck in your next hunt."*

Amazed, Richard watched as the dragon passed the deer across to their side of the canyon and deposited the animal gently unto its feet and released it to walk off on wobbly legs.

Still stunned to what he had just beheld, Richard murmured to Fae, "This is no murderous marauder. My Lord, it's a marvellous being with a heart of gold!"

"And with super hearing!" he thought, as the dragon's gaze locked on their position. After a pause for consideration, it smoothly lowered its head to rest inches above the ground, jaws a dozen feet before Richard.

To Richard's dismay, Fae launched off his shoulder to hover before the dragon's eyes, and started scolding the beast.

A gurgling emitted from the dragon's throat, and laughter echoed in Richard's mind.

"This is amazing! A human who is not only complementary concerning a dragon, but one accompanied by a sprite lass ready to do battle to protect him!"

There was no threat imparted in the mental link, only good-natured humour. And how Richard and the dragon could converse this way was apparently surprising to the both of them.

"Easy now, sister sprite … Fae is it? No harm will come to, … Richard!"

To that communication by the dragon, the sprite landed upon the creature's snout and crossed her arms as she gave it a stern glance. She then fluttered back to take her regular position on her friend's shoulder.

"You, you know my name? And Fae's?" Richard asked.

"Yes." the mental reply answered. *"I can read the mind of other creatures, and converse with them, mind to mind. But you are the first human that I've been able to communicate with."* The dragon chuckled. *"Human minds are to dense or something. Usually they can't pick up when I try to converse with them. But your mind is as clear to communication as your friend here."*

"You picked out what my name is. I feel rude in just thinking of you as 'the dragon.' How should I address you?"

"Ah." the creature agreed. *"I suppose it would be like for me to be referring to you as 'that human.' I've never needed a name. How would you like to provide me with one?"*

A short pause was all that Richard required. "Drake! How does that sound to you? I've just come from Drakeholm."

"Considering drake and dragon are one and the same, it really makes little difference to me. But I sense that you find it appropriate. So, Drake it is."

Richard suddenly sobered. "Drake, if you can read my mind, then you must know why I am here."

"Oh yes." Drake replied. *"I also understand the conditions under which you have been forced to accept such a contract. And the conflict now in your heart."*

Down hearted and nearly in tears, Richard spoke out loud, "Even if there was some way that I could kill you, I don't think I could ever bring myself to do it! And I don't know that if I just didn't come back, whether Magnus won't take my failure out on Gee and Gorm."

"Well then." The dragon said matter-of-factly. *"We will just have to bring my head to King Magnus's court."*

"Hah?" Richard was totally confused. "I just said I would never kill you."

"You're not listening carefully." Drake chuckled. *"I said 'We.' If I fly you and Fae*

back to Drakeholm, then my head will still be connected to the rest of me."

Human and sprite caught on at the same time. They both laughed, and Fae latched onto Richard's neck as he leapt into the air with a triumphant whoop.

"Hey, wait a minute…?"

"You're curious as to why I was invisible, when Fae's invisibility spell didn't work on you. 'Spell' may be what's different, as that involves magic. My invisibility is just a natural camouflage to me, so technically it's not really magic."

That explanation totally flew over Richard's head.

"Don't think to much about it. You'll just hurt yourself." and the dragon chuckled.

*

It had just gotten dark when the wizard strolled into the light of the camp's three fires. "Listen up, all of you!" Richard bellowed out. "Come morning pack up and head home. I'll greet you at the castle!"

The soldiers were too stunned to question, let alone detain, the tall man who walked back into the night. The sound and gusts of gigantic flapping wings only emphasized that they all were not having the same bewildering dream.

Chapter Eighteen

For once Richard wished that Fae's magic worked on him. As he neared the throne room he would have loved for the sprite to turn him invisible, as she had done with Gorm. To have simply appeared out of thin air before Magnus upon his throne would have been a hoot! And it definitely would have enhanced his reputation as a wizard upon the Court.

But Fae was doing the next best thing. Herself invisible, she fluttered ahead of him, putting the sentries asleep. Richard simply followed the trail of snoring soldiers.

At the double doors that closed them off from their destination, he gave a huge shove that would have slammed the inner walls, if it were not for the pair of guards that muffled their impact. He struck a grandiose pose, head back and right arm extended to clutch his mace just below the head with the end of the handle planted on the floor. (Considering the deliberate damage he had inflicted on Queen Sionna's floorboards, he kept in mind that this may someday be his domicile.) He rather thought that the mace could represent a wizard's staff. Richard also liked the idea of "approaching" the royal monarch within his own throne room with a weapon in hand.

Rapping the butt of the handle once upon the wooden floor, he stepped into the chamber. Not that he needed to gain everyone's undivided attention, as the party within had already gone deathly silent upon the door's dramatic opening.

When the partially stunned guards finally emerged from behind the door panels and made to intercept the wizard, they dropped to the floor in mid-stride (complements of Fae). With that the crowd before Richard parted, leaving only open space separating him from the King sitting on his throne. Breaking into a big toothy smile, Richard strode into the chamber, and was immensely satisfied to witness Magnus's face pale as he approached. It also pleased the wizard that his friends were present, and by all appearances, had been well treated.

"W… W… Wizard!" the King stammered. "

Richard chuckled. "His head is in the courtyard outside that window behind you as we speak."

Magnus gave a quick glance over his shoulder at the stained glass and then back to the tall man. His face clouded with confusion. "You made good time?" as he tried to calculate the expected days of travel and such.

"Excellent time Sire. I had extraordinary assistance."

"Well … ah. Shall we go out and see it?"

"No need Your Majesty." Richard couldn't hold back a laugh. "I'll simply bring it in through the window."

The shock on Magnus's face made Richard laugh again.

"After all, I am a wizard." He then turned serious. "I do strongly suggest that you stand down here beside me though, and for everyone else to move out of the way as well." as he waved for those on the floor to do so.

The King nervously rose off of his throne, straightened his robes, and descended the dais. Once he reached Richard's side, he nervously turned to observe the window.

"Ready Drakie?" the wizard mentally called out.

"All set Richie!" came the silent reply.

"Hey!" Richard chuckled.

"You started it." the dragon mentally smirked.

The spectacular stained glass dragon began to glow from the outside, and steadily increased in intensity. That brought awed murmuring from those in attendance, but turned to gasps as the room temperature suddenly elevated — and the glass panels liquefied and literally splashed onto the dais. (*"So much for not damaging my new home."* Richard thought.)

An ear shattering roar reverberated from outside, and the dragon shoved his head through the opening.

"Nice entrance!" Richard mentally complemented.

"First impressions are important after all." Drake replied.

Richard caught Magnus as his knees went rubbery, and not so gently hauled him back onto his feet.

"Look it here Magnus. You bald faced lied to me." the wizard growled directly, into the King's face. "And don't try lying again. The dragon reads people's minds, and he can communicate with me."

"Richard! He thinks I have a stash of treasure and he wanted to collect it when I'm

dead," the dragon sent.

"You have a cave full of gold?" Richard sent back.

"I don't even have a cave. And no, I have no interest, let alone use, for the stuff."

Richard turned a nasty glare at Magnus. "You wanted me to kill the dragon so you could get his treasure?"

The King gasped.

"Forget it!" he said. "There is no treasure. And there never were any attacks on the local farmers. So leave the dragon alone!"

Richard waved Gorm over and handed him the mace so that he could get a hold of his travel sack and opened it. After some rummaging he smiled and withdrew a leather tube sealed with wax. From it he pulled out a lambskin document. Smiling wickedly at Magnus, "I do believe we have a contract to cash in on."

"But, but … you didn't kill the dragon!" the King squealed.

Giving a close scan of the document, Richard pointed out, "Says nothing of actually killing the dragon. Only that I had to bring back the dragon's head. Your wording, mind you." Waving towards Drake, "And there, Sire, is the dragon's head."

Wide-eyed, the King swallowed noisily.

"Ah, Richard." Drake interrupted.

"I'm on a role here Drake."

"As I'm picking up." the dragon acknowledged. *"The princess's hand in marriage is part of the deal?"*

That paused Richard.

"You may want to take a good look at her, … and your friend Gee."

The pair's hands were entwined together, and both looked downcast. When they noticed Richard's scrutiny they released their grip and turned away from each other guiltily.

"While you were away," Drake murmured in Richard's mind, *"the two came to be very close."*

"Oh." He sighed audibly, as well as mentally.

Eyeing the ceiling as he considered his options, he then returned his glare at Magnus.

"Okay then." he opened sternly. "I'll nullify the contract *'if'* and only *'if'* you consent before these witnesses the following demands, and after the terms have been put down into writing and signed by the both of us. Agreed?"

King Magnus peered up to meet the wizard's eyes. "What are your terms?"

"One." Richard ticked off a finger on one hand. "The dragon is declared a protected being, to be allowed to live freely without harassment, and any attempt on his life is punishable by death."

Magnus nodded. "Agreed."

"Two." a second finger. "Dwarfs are to be accorded equal status with humans and to also be allowed to live free of harassment. Crimes against them to be dealt with the same as any other human citizen of the realm."

"Agreed." The King again nodded.

"Three." Another finger. "The same is to apply for all types of Sprites as with Dwarf's and humans."

"Sprites?" Magnus questioned incredulously.

"Agreed?" Richard growled.

The King shrugged. "Agreed."

When Fae popped into existence, hovering a hand span before Magnus's nose, the King started and leapt backwards. She then fluttered back to Richard's shoulder.

"This is Fae, a Forest Sprite." he introduced. "A very dear friend of mine."

"Term Four." This time he planted his fists on his hips. "Should it be mutually agreeable to the pair, the hand of Princess Magnia is to be transferred to Sir Gee, making him your heir upon your demise."

This brought a gasp of surprise from all parties concerned.

Richard turned to his friend and the princess. "Is that okay with the both of you?"

Astonished, the couple simultaneously bobbed their heads.

"Good." And Richard laughed. "Now wave a thank you to the dragon for this one. And for goodness sakes, hold hands again before I change my mind!"

When King Magnus hesitated while glancing back and forth between the happily relieved couple, Richard gave the man a nudge. "Would you rather have me as a son-in-law?"

Magnus blinked, looked up at the man towering next to him, and broke out into a broad grin. "You have a point there, wizard." Extending his hand and shaking Richard's, "Agreed!"

The entire crowd erupted into cheers.

Chapter Nineteen

The year following the Wizard having brought the dragon to court proved to have been a productive one. The King had granted a tower as residence for Richard and his Sprite. Magnus figured that it elevated his reputation to have in court a Wizard who had "tamed" a dragon. (Drake resented that concept, but let it pass as being a human thing.) Initially Richard's new residence was somewhat "Spartanish," but under Fae's direction became quite homey.

Gorm elected to remain with his friends, and Magnus also set up a smithy for him next to Richard's tower. His first project was to manufacture a revamped suit of armour for Gee. He eliminated all the gaudy aesthetic elements, produced lighter plating yet with superior strength, while actually making the "tin can" comfortable to wear and more manoeuvrable. He then took on a trio of apprentices, including a nephew he sent for who had shown signs of sharing his own magical blacksmithing talents. The dwarf was a hard taskmaster, but a very talented teacher. Gorm detested how others considered apprentices as unpaid "lackeys" to do their grunt work. From day one they were put to learning the mysteries of forge and anvil work. It wasn't long before he had them crafting hunting knives in preparation for weapons production.

Richard also spent a lot of time with Gorm in his smithy. He took up an unofficial apprentice position, working on a couple of specialized projects. As with his mace, he provided Gorm with the concept of the crossbow, and it didn't take the dwarf long to figure out the inner workings and redrawing mechanism necessary to make the thing work. When they presented the King and Gee with a functional prototype, Magnus enthusiastically provided backing for the equipping of every soldier in the castle with the instrument. This also provided employment for carpenters to fashion the stalks and bolt shafts for this new weapon. The apprentices spent a portion of each day in producing the crossbow's mechanical components.

Richard viewed the crossbow as his contribution to help defend his new home. His next cooperative endeavour with Gorm was the construction of a simple printing press, with ambitions for a more productive moveable-type version. His long-term aspiration was the establishment of a public education system.

Fae initially spent some time with Richard by the forge, but had difficulty dealing with the noise. She eventually found her niche when she befriended the castle's gardeners. Under her tutelage, the precinct's trees and flowers flourished to the delight of the Princess, the other ladies of the court, and were even noted by Magnus himself.

Gee and his princess married within the month that Richard and her father formally signed the agreement that the wizard so artfully dictated for the nullification of the original "Dragon's Head Contract." With the approach of their first anniversary, Magnia was glowingly heavy with child, and Sir Gee gushingly in anticipation of being a father.

Drake had returned to his home back in the forested mountain range in the south, but flew in monthly to visit Richard and Fae. Their mental communication waned with distance, but there was still an emotional contact when the dragon flew near the edge of the foothills.

With all that had gone so well during his first year in attendance at Drakeholm, Richard was ready to declare that this will be his "happily ever after."

Unfortunately, that was not to be.

*

The first indication of trouble came with the arrival of a grimy and exhausted young farmer's boy who requested immediate audience before the King. Rumour of the lad's arrival spread throughout the castle like wildfire. By the time a pair of guards admitted the boy to the throne room, Richard and his friends had also joined King Magnus.

The King waved the waif foreword, but by the time he stumbled the length of the hall, the lad collapsed to his hands and knees. Richard lowered himself to one knee, and gently raised him to sit upon the thigh of his bent leg.

"What is it lad?" the wizard whispered. "Tell the King."

The boy leaned against Richard's chest. After taking in a dozen deep breaths, he seemed to regain some strength. "Sire!" he called out. "We've been attacked! A huge army marches from the north!"

"When did this happen?" King Magnus asked in a calm voice.

"Afternoon, two days ago, they first entered our fields. Father sent me to you as he gathered our family and ran to the forest to hide. I've been running since then to get here."

"Brave lad. Thank you." Magnus waved over a pair of squires. "Take him to a guest room. Feed and bathe him, and see him to a comfortable bed. Attend to whatever he desires." Then he addressed the boy. "Thank you again. Rest knowing that you have the respect and appreciation of your King."

"And the King's Wizard." Richard breathed into his ear.

After the farm-boy had been led away, King Magnus turned to Gee. "How long would you say we have before they arrive?"

"That depends on just how large the contingent of foot soldiers they have." his son-in-law replied. "They've had two days. With forced march, perhaps late tomorrow. Most likely the day after. Then figure on another day to prepare for a siege. We won't have enough time to call in the levies, but we can still send out for reinforcements while we hold a defensive stand behind our walls." Gee grinned as he glanced Richard's way. "I believe your crossbows will prove to be a nasty surprise to anyone looking to scale the walls."

Magnus sighed as he took in his son-in-law's assessment. "Thank you Gee. Please see to summoning those levies." Waving Richard forward, "Have you any suggestions good friend?"

"I've got a thought. I'll need you to call out all able-bodied men and even woman of the city, along with whatever axes and saws they may have. And as many horses that can be gathered. Hopefully I can call in the air force."

The King looked strangely at the wizard.

Richard just smirked at him. "I'll fill you in later, if things work out."

*

But things didn't seem to be working out for what Richard had in mind. He had climbed up his tower and faced out from its southern wall.

"Damn!" he exploded. "I can't reach Drake. So much for our aerial assault. I'll just have to keep coming up here and calling out as the people prepare, and hope he comes close enough."

"I have another idea that'll give your legs a break." Fae said as she patted his neck. "Unless you actually want the exercise?"

Richard's eyebrows lifted as he looked over her way. "What ya got?"

"I can communicate with Drake just as easily as you. I won't make it to the mountains in two days, but I may get close enough to touch minds." the sprite suggested.

"Fae," the wizard smiled, "you're a marvel. You know that?"

"Of course, but it's nice to hear it. Speaking of which …"

"Yes, and you are lovely as well!" Richard laughed.

"About time!" as she slapped his neck, and flew off and vanished.

*

It was three days and midmorning when the first squad of mounted knights emerged from the forest road to the north and cut left along the tree line, then right, and then left again as they continued to file out of the woods. It went that way for nearly an hour before the foot soldiers finally made their appearance, and they packed the meadows for a quarter of the way towards the city. And then came wagon after wagon of supplies that crowded behind the knights along the tree line. Following them came a handful of standard bearers, and finally more mounted knights who spread out and formed a protective bubble for the army's upper command.

Richard sat upon George at nearly half the distance between the city walls and the northern forest, his mace resting across his right shoulder. To his left was mounted Gorm, sporting his personally crafted war hammer. Gee, wearing the dwarf's specially designed armour and mounted on Rex, stood next to Richard's right - even though the wizard had protested his friend endangering himself when his wife was so close to delivering. And that was the extent of Drakeholm's welcoming committee to face this invading horde - along with the tangle of tree trunks, limbs and brush that formed a wall before them. The barrier stood five feet high, ten deep and extended in either direction back to the far forests.

As they waited, an armoured standard bearer displaying a white flag separated himself from the army's main body, accompanied by a soldier mounted upon a common horse. The pair hadn't gotten far before Richard incredulously exclaimed, "Bort?"

Once the parley party had reached the shrubbery barricade, they halted. "Hello there Richard!" Bort called. "Hi Sir Gee! Hey Gorm!

Richard nearly laughed, but caught himself. "Well met Bort. Considering it's you escorting the parley, I take it that it's Queenie Sionna behind all this mischief."

Even though the standard bearer wore full armour with a closed visor, it was obvious that he tensed at the "Queenie" slur.

"Hale Sir Lurt!" Gee greeted the other knight. "Still licking Sionna's boots I see!"

The other knight lowered the staff's tip a foot towards his ex-fellow companion, but then checked himself.

"Have I been rubbing off on you Gee?" Richard mouthed sideways to his friend.

The knight merely grinned as he maintained his steady stare at the fellow across the wall.

"Where did Sionna come up with so large an army?" Richard asked Bort.

"Well. Remember that mission the guys and I were on when we first met?"

Richard nodded.

"Queen Sionna was being courted by King Tanus next door. They wed a month after your departure, uniting the two realms. Unfortunately for Tanus, he passed away two months later."

"Surprise, surprise." Richard murmured.

"The surprise would be he lasted that long." Gorm put in.

"And what brings Sionna to come visiting?" Richard coaxed.

Bort laughed. "Word of a talented wizard by the name of Richard gaining employment at Drakeholm reached Queen Sionna's court shortly after King Tanus's demise. Let's just say that you have been in her thoughts ever since you so rudely departed, and after hearing that news, it has become a rather dark obsession of hers to drop in."

"Meaning?" the wizard prompted.

Bort coughed, clearing his throat. Pulling out and unrolling a parchment scroll. "Queen Sionna demands of King Magnus that he surrender one Wizard Richard to her service …" and he paused to cough again.

"Or?"

"Or the armies commanded by Queen Sionna will put every man, woman and child of the realm of Drakeholm to the sword." Bort nearly choked, and gasped out, "Richard! She's been letting her men warm up on whoever they managed to get their hands on during our way here!"

The faces of the three companions all went stern.

Sir Gee nudged his horse forward a few steps. "As heir and son-in-law to His Majesty, King Magnus, I'll answer in his stead. Tell her miscreant Queenie Bitch Sionna to royally go to Hell!"

The metal tip of the banner pole flared white, igniting the white flag attached to it – complements of Gorm, though the Bearer assumed it had been the wizard. The knight wheeled his charger and dashed back towards his line.

Bort looked over his shoulder and tracked his companion's progress. He then turned to meet Richard's eyes. "Oh bloody hell!" he snarled, dismounted and made his away over the barricade. Once across, the huffing "ex-soldier" of Queen Sionna glanced up at Richard and remarked, "What now boss?"

Richard chuckled, "First off, climb aboard." as he reached down and hefted Bort up behind him onto George. The three horses turned and began a leisurely pace back towards the city.

Shortly there was the blare of war horns and the roaring battle cry from thousands of throats.

After twenty strides the companions turned again to face the charging horde. At that point Fae materialized on Richard's shoulder, facing the amazed soldier. "Hi Bort!" she called to him, and then also regarded the oncoming masses.

As footmen and mounted knights closed on the wooden barrier, a fiery infernal ignited one end of the low wall and continued to the further tip. Mass confusion erupted among the oncoming army.

"Hi Richie!" a familiar mental greeting came clearly into the wizard's head.

"Hey there Drake!" he sent back. *"Was starting to get a little worried."*

"You know how I like to make an entrance."

Richard laughed. "You ham!" he yelled, and then returned his attention to Sionna's army.

The dragon suddenly materialized in the air behind the troops, roared and blasted flame above the charging forces. Panic erupted among the ranks. Drake took advantage of the situation, swooping down and scooping the Queen off of her war charger. He carried the stunned monarch over the heads of her army, and unceremoniously deposited the woman in a heap before Richard's horse. The heavy armour that encased her hindered Sionna's efforts to get up onto her feet. Drake, who had landed next to the Queen, casually reached out and jerked her up and propped the monarch into a standing position.

Sionna awkwardly managed to raise her visor and scanned those horsed before her. She gasped upon recognizing the trio.

In desperation, she cried out to Sir Gee, "My Love! Kill this monster!"

The knight chuckled. "Sorry queenie." and he tapped his gloved left hand above the ring finger. "I'm happily married."

Out of the blue, dark storm clouds closed off the sky at an amazing rate. Calm air whipped into a tempest, forcing everyone to brace themselves in order to remain on their feet or horseback. Lightening and thunder cracked near simultaneously overhead and a deluge of rain pelted down, drowning out the burning barrier.

"God no!" Richard breathed as a glowing blue curtain materialized before him next to the smoldering wall. "Not now, please."

"Richard!" Fae shouted in his ear. "It's your way home!"

Before he could respond, Drake repositioned himself, and in the process his tail flicked the Queen through the blue shimmer – and she vanished, along with the portal.

"*Oops!*" the dragon's apologetic mental voice sounded in Richard's head. "*Clumsy me!*" And he laughed.

*

The remaining commanders of the defeated army sued for peace before Sir Gee and his Wizard and Dwarf friend – backed by the humongous dragon exhaling smoke. Those knights enthralled by Sionna's spell had been released from her control, which also contributed to the mass accord to surrender.

Gee whispered aside to Richard, "What do we do now?"

Richard turned to his friend and raised both hand with palms open his way. "Don't look at me. I avoided politics by pawning all this off onto you. But it looks as if your father-in-law just won himself a bigger kingdom." Smiling, "Let's let him deal with it!"

112

Chapter Twenty

It took three days for King Magnus to negotiate a peace accord. Not that there was any real dispute. Those nobles originally of King Tanus's realm were never all that eager to bow down and pledge allegiance to their new Queen (especially following the suspicious passing of their sovereign so soon after the wedding). Sionna's own nobility were accustomed to her idiosyncrasies, and basically stepped in line because she scared the hell out of them. As for her bewitched boy-toy knights, once her presence in this world became non-existent, the spell was broken, making them wonder what they ever saw in her — many requested leave to return home with assurances that they would behave themselves.

As a whole, the entire army was in awe of a King who had a wizard in his service who could open a portal to another world and command a dragon — especially with the beast still in attendance, curled up and snorting smoke in the space between the city and where they were camped. There was also the occasional crossbow practice in the same area, which provided a constant background noise of steel tipped bolts punching through breast-plated targets. This unusual weapon with its devastating capability provided another motivational demonstration for the new comers to cooperate. It was common consensus that they would rather be in an alliance with such a King rather than risk coming to blows with him.

In the end King Magnus declared that each realm would be granted independence for the price of a yearly tribute payable to his kingdom. The nobility of each would select a new monarch who will pledge a peace pact with Drakeholm, and each other.

The declaration by King Magnus took only the first day, and that was with a victory banquet for all the nobility that evening. The next two days were occupied by the choosing of the new monarchs — during which there was a flurry of debating, along with the mysterious disappearance of some candidates. By the end of the final day all had been resolved, pledges given, and another party.

Both Wizard and King's son-in-law had made themselves scarce during the whole affair. To be fair, Richard did have other things on his mind. However, he did remain in residence during the whole affair, in case things got difficult for the King, but his time was occupied stewing over a personal matter.

The morning after the final peace party and the foreign guests were making ready to depart back to where they belonged, Richard had made up his mind to act.

"Fae." Richard murmured to the sprite. "I think we need to pay a visit to your father. I'd like to know if the Earth Stone has been acting up again."

"I've been wondering about that myself?" she admitted. "If it was the stone, I'm sorry it came at a bad time and you missed your way home."

"Took you long enough, knuckle head!" Drake communicated on a private brain length. *"And of course I'll fly the two of you there, just in case you didn't come up with that idea yourself."*

*

Richard spent the rest of the morning arranging their departure. He let King Magnus, Gee and Gorm know of his intent and wasn't sure how long he would be away. The King gave no argument. Gorm bid him good luck. Gee just pressed the point that they'd better be back before Magnia delivered. It was Bort that Richard spent a good deal of time with, requesting that the soldier undergo a special mission for him, and went into a great amount of detail about it.

By the finish of the midday meal, Richard and Fae boarded the "Drake Express" and took to the air. Following Fae's directions he had the pair to their destination before sunset. The dragon touched down at the Earth Stone clearing, as it was the largest open space in the vicinity. He had also taken it upon himself to make a public broadcast to the local sprites of the pair's imminent arrival, and by the time he landed, the entire sprite community were crowded around the rock's clearing.

"Hello, daughter!" Bower called out.

"Daddy!" the sprite cried, and flew to his open arms.

"Welcome to you too Richard, and the dragon as well." her father added.

"My, you do make odd friends, wizard."

"You haven't seen the half of them." Drake communicated.

"Bower, this is Drake." Richard introduced. "A most welcome friend, and someday I'd like you to meet the others that he's hinted about. And I'm assuming that Drake has already filled you in as to why we're here."

The dragon chuckled and the sprite leader smiled as he nodded his head in acknowledgement.

The growing gloom suddenly began to pulse with a bluish glow radiating from the engraved runes upon the Earth Stone.

"It's started again." Bower breathed.

Richard's stomach took on a leaden sensation as he noticed that the glow matched the blue of the portal that had brought him here. "Is this the first since my arrival?"

"No." the sprite replied. "It started again nearly a month ago, and finished a few days back." He glanced at his daughter and back to Richard. "I was afraid that it might of drawn you through."

"Nearly did, but Drake took care of that." But before the sprite could ask, "We'll fill you in on all of that later." Nodding towards the Earth Stone. "And this?"

"Just started again, but more intense than it normally begins with."

The dragon eyed the glowing monolith, then reached out with his giant paw and gripped the stone.

A collective gasp escaped from the crowd of sprites, and Richard inhaled with surprised apprehension.

Nothing happened.

"Interesting." Drake exclaimed. *"The rock is attuned to you Richard."* After more consideration, *"The thing is not evil. If anything, it just wants to look after you. The Stone wants to know your heart's desire."*

"What?" the human questioned.

"It's simply asking that you touch it and concentrate upon your heart's desire." The dragon explained.

"But if I...?"

"As I said, it is attuned to you. Your 'non-magic' will not affect it. Simply place your hands on the stone and think about what you wish most for."

On a mental wavelength, Richard confided with his friend. *"That would involve another. What if it's not reciprocal? I don't want to risk harming another."*

"Make know your wish to the Stone. It will not force a contradiction to someone else's

wishes."

Cautiously Richard raised and placed his palms against the glowing engraved surface. It was surprisingly a comforting sensation. Closing his eyes he surrendered his thoughts of what he longed for.

The eruption of gasps and awes compelled him to pull back and glance around. To his stunned amazement, Fae stood beside him – nearly his own height! Her wings were no longer present. "Oh, Fae! I didn't mean …"

But she didn't give Richard the chance to finish, rapping her arms around his neck and silencing him with a sound kiss. By the time she relaxed her grip and backed off to smilingly stare into his eyes, he came to the realization it wasn't just his own wish having been granted.

Thoughts of another came to mind. "Bower?" and he glanced around. When he spotted Fae's father, his fears dissipated upon seeing the sprite also smiling.

"What?" the elder sprite shrugged. "You think any father would be angry seeing his daughter so happy?"

Turning back to the now human Fae, he gently clasped her hands and proceeded to complete what he wished. Dropping to one knee and gazing up to her face, "Fae, I love you. Will you marry me?"

An impish grin crossed her lips. "Perhaps?"

Richard laughed, "Fae. You are Awesome and Lovely!"

"Of course!" she replied. "And that also goes for marrying you!"

*

The pair agreed upon a human ceremony once they returned to Drakeholm, but to Fae's surprise, Richard consulted with Bower as to what was necessary to have a sprite wedding while they were here. Normally the sprite leader would conduct such an event, but being the father of the bride, another sprite elder would officiate. Or, in this case, the honour was shared by Snowdrop and Sage. It took two days of preparation, and the happy couple were united on the third. "Spriteful" celebrations followed to extend far into the night.

Chapter Twenty-One

Fae and Richard remained in Home for another week, visited by friends and family of the ex-sprite. Drake made himself comfortable next to the Earth Stone. He was a great curiosity to the sprites that peppered the dragon with questions about himself. The youngsters entertained themselves using the huge creature as a playground, and Drake was more than pleased to oblige them.

Finally the happy couple announced their intent to leave, as Richard had another visit in mind. They promised to make further visits in the future. Drake voiced that he would see that they kept that promise, and would provided the transportation himself – so that he could also visit.

It was a short flight to the way station belonging to Sendra and her family.

*

Tina and Sendra were occupied giving the front porch a thorough scrubbing as movement in the yard caught the mother's eye. Expecting a new-come traveler to the way station, she looked up, to be surprised by a man and woman hand in hand, casually strolling her way. A brilliant smile flashed with the recognition of the fellow, and she whispered her daughter's name.

Sendra looked up, wondering what her mother had in mind, and exploded in a flurry of work dress, mop and toppled bucket as she flew off the porch and charged into the open hands of Richard who scooped the child up into a welcoming embrace.

By the time Tina had made her way to greet the couple, Richard had her daughter perched upon his hip. The older woman hugged him and gave Fae a curious, but welcoming, eye. As Richard inhaled to introduce his companion, Tina raised her hand to indicate him to wait.

"Thomas! Get your hide out here! We have Guests!"

It took but a moment for the farmer to exit through the stable door, confused as to why his wife would interrupt his chores to greet way station visitors. His expression transformed to delight upon glancing Richard, and his pace quickened as he hurriedly wiped his hands on his shirttails. Once within reach, their hands clasped – and Thomas gazed in awe as he first looked upon the "tall" fair lady standing on Richard's far side.

"Tina, Thomas, Sendra." Richard nodded to each. "This is Fae, my wife!"

The trio as one took an intake of air that returned in whoops and greetings of congratulations. Tina swooped in to exchange hugs, and Sendra leaned over from Richard's hip to be transferred to Fae's embrace.

Having heard the commotion from the far side of the barn, Marth dashed around the corner on the run, followed shortly by another individual. On seeing that there was no emergency, she slowed to a breathless walk – and then dashed again upon recognizing Richard. As for the man, he froze in place with the look of horror on his face.

Richard hugged the young woman, as he gave a hard eye to the familiar figure.

Hal twitched as if about to bolt, but Thomas laughed and waved him forward. The fellow remained in place, but at least his apprehension diminished some.

"All's well wizard." The farmer explained. "He's been doing a proper courting to Marth for nearly the past year."

Sendra squirmed down, purposely walked over to Hal and led him by the hand to face Richard (who was having a hard time not to laugh).

"Hello Hal." Richard greeted. "Seeing's that you're still alive, I take you've been behaving yourself."

Hal's eyes bulged with the reminder of the wizard's curse. When Richard gave him a big grin, he finally relaxed and returned a shy smile.

The clip clop of a number of horses coming up the lane brought the merry group to silence. "Darn!" Tina snorted. "Of all the times for travellers to be dropping by."

"It's okay Tina." Richard soothed. "I've actually arranged for another friend to show up."

As Richard had expected, Bort rode around the final laneway bend, leading George on a tether. On one side of the soldier was mounted Gorm, and on the other rode a woman the wizard had never seen before.

Upon spying their friend, Gorm and Bort nudged their animals into a canter, having dropped George's line and letting him and the lady to come along at a more leisurely pace.

"Hey Boss!" Bort called as the pair pulled up. "We're here!"

"We it is." Richard welcomed with a surprised smile at the dwarf.

"Caught this one scrounging around, making ready to disappear with George. So I convinced him to let me tag along."

"What about the apprentices?"

"They know enough to do what needs doing." the dwarf huffed. "I put my nephew in charge and he'll make sure of it."

By this time George approached Richard and leaned his forehead into his shoulder. Taking the horse's tether, he handed the rope to a surprised Thomas.

"I don't get around to riding George much anymore. I was hoping you could give him a good home."

The farmer scratched between the horse's ears, prompting George to nuzzle into him. Thomas laughed. "Yeah. I think we'll get along quite well. Thank you."

"Thank you." Richard responded.

The wizard now gazed up at the unfamiliar woman on her horse. "Hello there…?"

"This is Daisy." Bort introduced, and assisted her out of her saddle. "She's the reason I couldn't leave Sionna's service when you, Gorm and Sir Gee hightailed it out of her palace. Gorm here consented to letting me stop by to pick her up to meet you. We'll grab a wagon on the way back for her things."

"Softy!" Richard jeered at the dwarf.

"Shut up Richie." Gorm growled, then chuckled.

"But anyways." Bort continued. "Once we get settled in Drakeholm, we're hoping to get married."

"In that case." Fae stepped forward to take Daisy's hand. "Maybe we can arrange a double ceremony."

Seeing the ex-sprite for the first time; "Fae?" Bort gawked. Then, clearing his throat. "You've grown!"

The tall couple laughed, and the ex-sprite suggested, "A story we'll get to as we sit around tonight."

"We've already been married before Fae's family and friends," Richard explained, "but are planning on a second ceremony back in Drakeholm."

Daisy spoke up for the first time. "We will be honoured to join in with your wedding."

"*Ah-hem!*" sounded in Richard's head.

"And I've just been reminded." (As Richard sent back, *"I thought dragons were supposed to be patient?"*) "I've got one more friend to introduce." (*"Where are you anyways?"*)

"Right behind you." the mental answer came.

"Walking are you? Sneak!" Richard mentally replied, and then laughed. *"Did you know about Gorm and Daisy?"*

"Of course." the dragon replied, and he snickered.

To Daisy, Thomas and his family, "Please, I would like to introduce a friend to myself and Fae, as well as to Gorm and Bort."

As Richard turned with a swoop of his hand, the family and Daisy were bewildered to find the open space between themselves and the barn empty.

"This," Richard waved, "is Drake."

And the dragon materialized, curled up on his belly, wings folded along his back, and chin resting on the ground.

All but Sendra gasped. The girl squealed, "He's amazing!" and dashed up to hug (as best she could) the dragon's enormous snout.

Drake chuckled and broadcast to Richard and Fae, *"She's amazing too!"*

Sendra turned back to the others and gleefully cried, "Drake said I was amazing too!"

The dragon raised his head and stared down in surprise at the child, as Fae and Richard also looked upon her in awe.

Together the couple strolled over to the girl.

"Sendra," Richard knelt down before the lass, "how would you like to go for a ride with us on Drake?"

Ice: More Than Meets The Eye

By R. G. Berg

Luanne glanced out her dorm window. Even though she couldn't see the full moon poised somewhere above her, it illuminated the snow and forest before her nearly as well as the winter sun would have. Better, actually, with its soft, comforting light. The past hour's concentration on her Language Arts project had strained her eyes, so the calming view outside provided a soothing balm for them.

A click and whoosh announced to Luanne's ears that the door to her townhouse residence had been opened. She recognized the giddy laughter to belonging to Emily, her friend and housemate. Luanne wasn't expecting her back from the Leap Year Pub this early. Unfortunately, Luanne perceived that Ems was not alone. One, no two male voices. "Please Ems." she breathed. "Not tonight. There's so much more I want to get done."

"Hey Ice!" accompanied Emily's banging on Luanne's closed door. "What ya up to?"

Ice was Luanne's appointed nickname, though few besides Emily applied it in a friendly manner. Luanne was an albino, white hair, white skin, pink irises and all. It freaked most people out. Ems was one of the few exceptions.

Not bothering for an answer, Emily burst through the door. "Come on Ice!" she slurred. She wasn't plastered, but just a bit past being happily tipsy. "I've got a surprise for you!"

"Ems, I've got stuff to get done. And I'm not interested in meeting some guy you found for me at that pub."

It was Emily who looked surprised. "How'd you know?"

Luanne tilted her head with an expression that conveyed, *How do you think?"*

"Oh, well. But these guys are just so cool! They want to go for a walk on the trails in the dark!"

"So?"

"I know, you do that thing all the time. But it'll be something new to me."

"You could have come anytime with me."

"Well, ah. This'll be with guys!"

Luanne rolled her eyes, and closed them as she passed her left hand down that side of her face to rest against here cheek.

"Hey! What's keeping you?"

The two girls turned to the man standing in the room's doorway. A second male's head peered from around the doorframe. Luanne assessed the pair with a single glance, and disliked them instantly. They gave her the creeps.

"Oh, this is Jack." Emily indicated the fellow who had spoken, a tall, lean dude with long blond hair protruding from beneath a Habs toque. "And Ryan." who leered at Luanne with a gap-toothed grin. What she could make out from his dark haired roundish head, he stood about average height with likely a heavy-set build. Both were definitely too old to be attending a university social gathering.

"Do you mind?" Luanne snapped. "A little privacy please!"

The two stepped a pace down the hall.

"Farther! Like the front door! Now!" She waited until she could hear them tramp to the indicated location.

Smoothly Luanne rose and moved to the door and closed it, then leaned her back against the barrier. As she glared at her friend, "Are you out of your mind?"

"They were so nice, and Jack's so cute …"

"And they bought you drinks?"

"Yeah."

"And listened to you talk?"

"Well … yeah. And they got really interested in meeting you!"

"You told them about me?"

Emily began to squirm.

"That your friend is an albino?"

Suddenly Emily found the Gandalf poster next to the door very fascinating. "Ah, yeah."

"And you didn't think it a little creepy that they wanted to meet the local freak, and drag us off into the woods at night?"

With a shrug, "Not really. It just kind of sounded …"

"Romantic?"

"No, well. Thrilling? Adventurous?"

"Try insane. A bad idea."

"But …" Emily's features transformed into a pout. "I take that's a no?"

"You got it."

"Then I'm going anyways."

"Then you are insane."

"Don't care!" Emily retorted defiantly. "It just seems so neat!"

Luanne closed her eyes as she brought her head back to rest against the door, and took a deep, slow breath. "Okay, okay. I must be insane too. I'll go." Then turned a stern glare at her friend. "But if they so much as lay a finger on either of us, we're out of there."

*

A quarter of an hour later the foursome were crossing the walkway-topped dam that held back the frozen pond backing the western precincts of the joint university/college complex. Just beyond that structure laid the snow-carpeted forest. As they left the dam and the poled-lighting that illuminated the walkway, Jack and Ryan pulled flashlights from their coat pockets and switched them on.

Luanne stopped dead in her tracks. "Turn them off."

In unison they swung their lights into Luanne's face, to which she turned away and covered her eyes with her gloved hands.

"Turn them off!" she snapped.

"What's your problem?" Jack snarled.

"For one, you nearly blinded me. For another, you're better off without the lights."

Before either guy could start arguing, Emily spoke up. "Just do it. Luanne does this in the dark all the time. Do as she says and see."

Reluctantly the lights went out.

"Now wait." Luanne instructed. "Give your eyes a chance to adjust."

In a short while her demand became literally clear. The full noon did its part. To the astonishment of the other three, they were able to distinctly make out the trees, snow, the beaten paths, and each other.

"With the snow on the ground" Luanne explained, "and the leaves off the trees, you can see quite well, even without the moon being full. Those flashlights just create excess shadows and cancel out your night vision, throwing off your perception. You would be stumbling all over the place, and likely end up face first in the snow."

Emily was gleefully impressed, Jack and Ryan grudgingly, and silently, so.

Jack took the lead, followed by Emily, then Luanne, with Ryan trailing behind. To no surprise to Luanne, Jack took the Lookout Trail. It was likely the most popular walking path, even though it was the steepest. She was relieved that he didn't head for one of the cross-country ski trails. That would have sparked another dispute.

Initially Emily chattered merrily as they made their way up the hill, but eventually fell quiet as neither of the men responded to her talk. Luanne remained silent herself, finding it unsettling that Em's new found buddies failed to respond to her attempts at conversation.

At the summit it was Luanne who pointed out the wooden structure that overlooked frozen Lake Nipissing, and insisted that they stop to take in the view. Perhaps Jack wasn't as familiar with the trails as he made out that he was, but the notion that he may have deliberately chosen to bypass the lookout put Luanne all the more on her guard.

It wasn't long before Jack called for a continuance of their walk. He soon turned right onto a path that squeezed between a pair of hemlock trees. Luanne was acquainted with the trails up here, but this one was new and unknown to her. She did not like what she was suspecting. The path dipped, crowded by numerous other evergreens, and then turned upwards again to open upon a flat, bald hilltop. All during the traipsing of this path Luanne's hackles were aroused, and she prepared herself for trouble. Her senses had picked up the barest hint of blood, perhaps suppressed by the cold, but she wasn't sure if she was just imagining it. When Luanne crested the rim of the hill she was not surprised to discover that she had been correct.

The packed snow had been lined out with blood, goat from the closer scenting. A quick glance suggested a pentagram outlined from tip to tip by a circle. They had entered the clearing from the south, greeted by the first tip of the star, the next two protruded to the east and west, the further pair marked out northeast and north west.

"Damn!" she mentally cursed. *"These idiots think they're Satanists!"*

Her appearance over the rim also sparked a flurry of activity. Jack turned and lunged for Emily, dragging her to the ground. Ryan attempted a dash up the remainder of the slope, only to be greeted by a back kick in the chest from Luanne, launching him back down the trail. During this Jack had managed to secure Emily back onto her feet, with her left arm hammer locked behind her. Nine inches of steel glinted moonlight at her throat.

"Don't scream!" Jack snarled as he backed his victim to the centre of the pentagram. "And don't even think of running or I'll slit her throat."

"Wouldn't think of it." Luanne cocked her right eyebrow and returned his glare with a cold, barely perceivable smile.

Jack found it difficult to maintain eye contact, but dared not break it.

"Come here and kneel before me!" he demanded, but his voice cracked before he could finish. "Ryan! Get the hell up here, damn you!"

Her smile crinkled just a hair broader as she took her first step forward, peeling off her left glove as she came. Eyes locked on Jack's, she didn't so much as blink.

A shiver ran up Jack's back. He recalled the albino's nickname, "Ice," and it crossed his mind that there may be a significant truth behind it.

A sudden dead weight slumped against his chest and Jack discovered that Emily had passed out. He managed to shift the grasp of his left arm to the centre of her coat between her shoulder blades and dragged her backwards enough so that her knees locked to take some of the weight.

While Jack accomplished this, Luanne had taken three more slow steps, having removed her other glove and slid out of her white coat.

For some reason it hadn't clued in to Jack before this that Ice had been decked out all in white. Even her thigh high mukluk-style boots where white. The shiver that ran up his spine now permeated his whole body. Jack's arms and hands began to shake, threatening to nick Emily with his knife.

And still Ice came. Two paces between them, and Luanne broke the chill night's silence. "You want to play with magic? You haven't a clue what you were getting into." A final stride and she casually reached up to grasp the naked blade with her left hand, wrapping her fingers around it, protecting Emily's exposed throat from its edge.

As if suddenly shaken out of a trance, Jack jerked hard on the knife. He felt the edge bite into flesh, but Ice didn't even flinch. A burst of stars dazzled his vision just before all went dark, followed by a sensation of weightlessness.

Luanne's right palm was still open as she pulled back from smacking the creep in the forehead. Emily's body crumpled to the ground, but before Jack did the same, Luanne latched onto the front of his coat. The knife was still imbedded across her left inner hand, but he no longer had a grip on it. Behind her she could hear Ryan scrambling into the clearing. Luanne grinned wickedly, pivoted to her left and flung shot put style to launch Jack towards where Ryan stood. He nearly made the distance.

The shock of landing face first in the trampled snow jarred Jack out of his stupor. Groggily he pushed himself onto his hands and knees, looking up to find Ryan starring past him in shock. Too shaky to stand, Jack managed to roll over onto his backside, propped up with both arms behind him. There stood Ice, a protective pace between them and Emily's supine form. And then she started walking their way.

"So you wanted magic?" She raised her bleeding hand still clutching the blade. "I'll show you magic." She released the knife and let it fall to the snow. In the pale moonlight Luanne's blood gleamed a stark black against the vivid whiteness of her skin. During the next stride the deep laceration closed as they watched and all stain of blood was absorbed without a trace.

Eyes locked on her assailants, Luanne leaned forward and extended her left hand towards the ground. Before it contacted the snow, it had transformed into a white paw.

Jack and Ryan stared in terror at the massive white wolf coming at them. In panic the two men careened into each other, loosing their bearings. Jack dashed off west, and Ryan blindly followed. With a deep-throated growl, the lupine padded after the pair.

*

The next morning Emily awoke in her own bed. She was groggy and had a hard time thinking. "What did I do last night?" she grumbled into her pillow. "God, my head hurts. Did I drink that much?"

A short time later, there was a knock at her door, and Luanne entered without being invited. "Morn'n sleepy head. Got some tea and toast for you, but drink this water first."

Emily cracked an eye open and cringed. "Go away!" she groaned. "I'm dying!"

Not a chance, on either account. I'm here to raise the dead. Besides, this is payback from last night, even if you can't remember what for."

"Just what did I do?"

"Never mind. If it's that much of a blur, you're probably better off not knowing."

"Oh, by the way, you've missed the big news of the morning. Two out-of-towners who were at that pub last night ended up in Duchesnay Creek. Washed up where the water is open below the falls."

"Now drink!"

Additional Books by R. G. Berg

Wolf Shield

If the love of your life had been horrendously murdered, what would you do? For the "werewolf," Ralph, there was but one course of action – hunt down and destroy the vampire responsible! The blood lusting Flannery may change his form and name over the centuries, but his foul scent would forever mark him. For nearly two millennia the deadly pursuit for vengeance would weave through the British Isle, Continental Europe, and even onto the New World. In the end there could only be one survivor in this deadly game of cat and mouse between these two immortal entities.

Wolf Shield - Progenies

The werewolf, Ralph, is in vengeful hot pursuit for the vampire that was responsible for the horrid death of his pregnant wife. Unbeknownst to the shape shifter, he is also being tracked; by his grown twin offspring he was unaware had miraculously survived their mother's killing. The brother and sister are to face their own battles with an assortment of evils upon the journey to find their sire.

Author's Biography

R. G. Berg self-published *Wolf Shield* in 2008. It has since been re-edited a number of times since. Although *Wolf Shield* had initially been intended as a standalone work, with much prompting from readers, a parallel companion work titled *Wolf Shield – Progenies* has been published. He has also contributed a short story, *Ice*, to an anthology titled *THE PECULIAR FULL MOON*, compiled by a local author's group: themed in regards to a full moon in conjunction with February 29th. Despite the collection's reference to the positioning of our orbiting satellite, *Ice* follows within the premise that "shape shifters" have no cursed affiliation to full moons.

Even though Berg had been christened as the "Werewolf of Edward's Hall" by his residence mates at McMaster University, he resented that the title tended to have some negative connotations.